I hope you enjoy reading my book.

The Time of the Remnant

Rebecca Galloway Grice

All rights reserved. No part of this publication may be reproduced, distributed, or transmitted in any form or by any means, including photocopying, recording, or other electronic or mechanical methods, without the prior written permission of the publisher, except in the case of brief quotations embodied in critical reviews and certain other noncommercial uses permitted by copyright law. For permission requests, write to the publisher, TEACH Services, Inc., at the address below.

Copyright © 2020 Rebecca Galloway Grice

Copyright © 2020 TEACH Services, Inc.

ISBN-13: 978-1-4796-1248-2 (Paperback)

ISBN-13: 978-1-4796-1249-9 (ePub)

Library of Congress Control Number: 2020912098

All Scripture quotations are taken from the KING JAMES VERSION (KJV): KING JAMES VERSION, public domain.

"Jesus Is Coming Again." Hymn #213. *The Seventh-day Adventist Hymnal.* Hagerstown, MD: Review and Herald Publishing Association, 1985.

Maxwell, Arthur S. *The Bible Story.* Vol. 1–10. Washington, DC: Review and Herald Publishing Association, 1953–1957.

White, Ellen G. *The Triumph of God's Love.* Washington, DC: Review and Herald Publishing Association, 1950.

Dedication

This book is dedicated to my late husband, Elder Clay Grice, pastor, publishing director, and literature evangelist trainer.

This book is also dedicated to all the other faithful men, women, and youth who have spent countless hours spreading the gospel through the printed page.

Table of Contents

INTRODUCTION 7

THE STOLTZFUS FAMILY

Chapter One	Encounter with Rachel	10
Chapter Two	A Visit from the Brethren	15
Chapter Three	Church Meeting	20
Chapter Four	Troubles with Eli	26
Chapter Five	A Miracle for Julie	51
Chapter Six	A Family Gathering	57
Chapter Seven	Decision	45
Chapter Eight	A Warning	51
Chapter Nine	The Letter	54

THE WEBSTER FAMILY

Chapter Ten	Midnight in Mississippi	61
Chapter Eleven	A Gray Morning	67
Chapter Twelve	The Blue Book	72

THE STOLTZFUS FAMILY

Chapter Thirteen	Apprehension	77

THE WEBSTER FAMILY

    Chapter Fourteen   Homeless 84

    Chapter Fifteen   Mrs. Mattie Johnson 88

THE STOLTZFUS FAMILY

    Chapter Sixteen   Mary 94

    Chapter Seventeen   Asteroid 101

THE WEBSTER FAMILY

    Chapter Eighteen   Mrs. Mattie's Church 107

    Chapter Nineteen   Jerusalem 110

    Chapter Twenty   Mrs. Mattie's Stand 111

THE STOLTZFUS FAMILY

    Chapter Twenty-One   In Lancaster County 115

THE REMNANT FAMILY

    Chapter Twenty-Two   Waiting and Praying 121

    Chapter Twenty-Three   He Comes! 127

Introduction

For generations, the Stoltzfus family had lived a quiet life surrounded by friends and fellow Mennonite church members. Eli Stoltzfus knew the Mennonites had come to Pennsylvania because of their desire to live in peace and to worship in the way they believed was right.

But things were changing—there was trouble throughout the world and, with each catastrophe, people were becoming more fearful. The Concerned Citizen's Council began innocently enough in the nineties as a grassroots organization of clergy and civic leaders intent on putting pressure on the public to elect and then demand moral accountability from those in public office. As new problems occurred throughout the world, the CCC became more powerful, until it had become the ultimate authority on moral and civil law.

Now the Stoltzfus's family doctor was being treated like a criminal. All he'd ever done was help others and take a stand for what he believed was right—and that was the right to worship on the day he chose. *Isn't that what America is all about—being free to follow your own beliefs?* Eli reasoned. Suspicion of everyone and everything had wedged its way into their lives and stayed like an uninvited guest.

Throughout earth's history, there have been men and women who valued the truth of God's Word above their own lives. They have stood firm in their beliefs before kings, dictators, governments, and religious leaders.

Eli and his family had always been obedient to God's Word, as they understood it, but now new understanding had come to Eli. A seed of truth had been planted in his heart by books he had purchased from a salesman years earlier—truth he had hidden until now.

As Jesus's second return looms closer and the circumstances on earth become desperate, will Eli make the decision to stand for what he knows is right? Will his family stand with him?

Around the world, people are being called to stand with God's remnant people. Will they choose what is right or will they harden their hearts? The seeds have been sown by faithful workers for God—now it is time for the harvest.

THE STOLTZFUS FAMILY

Chapter One

Encounter with Rachel

Sarah looked up from the kitchen sink, as a wind gust shook the leaves of the oak by the kitchen window. The wind gathered speed, forming a dust devil as it swept across the yard and into the adjacent field where it rattled the dry corn stalks.

Wiping the beads of perspiration from her brow, she surveyed the kitchen. Everything was tidy again. The dishes were put away, floor swept, counters scrubbed. Cleaning was easier now that there was just Eli and her to share the evening meal. She remembered how busy it had been when all four of the Stoltzfus children were home.

Eli and she had taught their children well. Hard work and being responsible were part of their Mennonite tradition. The training had begun with simple chores when the children were young. Eli had taught the boys to help with the farm, tending the crops, milking and taking care of the herd, and Sarah had the responsibility of teaching the girls.

> *Hard work and being responsible were part of their Mennonite tradition*

In her mind's eye, Sarah could see Eli and the boys working together—Tom, the oldest son, tall and dark like his father, and Jonathan, only two years younger, sandy-haired with intense blue eyes. Eli would look at Jonathan, shake his head and say, "Sarah, it should have been one of the girls who got your eyes. Those eyes remind me of an October sky." As they grew older, the boys were given more and more responsibility on the farm so that Eli could take over the family's grocery store and farmer's market.

Grandfather Stoltzfus was getting older and Eli would, as expected, take over running the business.

Sarah missed the time she'd shared with the girls as they had busied themselves with household chores. Bubbly, happy-go-lucky Mary always had something to tell that would make them laugh.

"Mary, why do these things always happen to you?" Rachel, the oldest of the Stoltzfus children often asked. "I worry about you."

Sarah remembered telling Eli, *"Rachel is so good; I don't think I deserve a child like her."*

Still reminiscing, Sarah recalled asking Eli, *"Do you know that she picked out her very best dress and her favorite doll to give to Rebecca Martin when their house burned? She was too shy to take them up to the front in the church where they were gathering things for the Martin family. She had Mary take them up for her."* "What did Mary give?" Eli had questioned.

"A smile and something she had long since discarded. But you know Mary, she had Rebecca and the other children laughing and playing, when just a short time before they'd all been sitting around bemoaning their loss. I think even Hannah Martin took pleasure in seeing her children being happy."

Sarah glanced in the small mirror that hung over the sink. She wiped away the beads of perspiration from her forehead and carefully tucked a stray wisp of unruly hair back under the small cap that sat on the crown of her head. Deep in thought, she stepped outside onto the porch. The family dogs, Rags and Little Bit, both raised their heads and looked up. Little Bit, the more energetic of the two, bounded up the steps to Sarah. She sat on the porch swing and absentmindedly stroked his head.

Rachael could not have known, but there was a reason to worry. Blond, curly-haired Mary had always been a ray of sunshine in their lives, but perhaps Sarah should have seen that trouble was coming. Beneath Mary's cheerfulness, there lurked a restlessness that Sarah could not understand. All of their children had done well in the small, church-operated school they attended, but, unlike Rachel, housework, cooking, and gardening hadn't appealed to Mary. Working at the family's market was the only thing that interested her, and it was there that Mary had shone. Customers were drawn to her quick smile and willingness to help.

The late afternoon sun rays cast a golden glow on the land and reflected off of the windows of the large, sturdy barn where Eli and Jonathan were finishing the milking. At times, Sarah could hear their voices rising above the lowing of the cows and the clanking of the milking equipment.

Sarah watched as a flock of Canadian geese flew low over the fields, looking for a resting place. She felt that familiar hurt inside—hard and grating, like the dried kernels of corn stored in the barn—when she thought of how it had happened. If only that Jason Carter hadn't caught Mary's fancy. He was an Englishman—not one of them. Mary had met him while working at the market. Eli had been furious with the questions Mary had begun to ask, "Why do we do this?" or "What's wrong with that?" Questions that seemed to undermine their Mennonite heritage. Perhaps they should have been more patient with her and careful with their answers, but her questions had been disturbing. Sarah could still see Mary's pained expression when Eli had forbidden her to work at the market or see Jason again.

The day that Mary left was only one moment in Sarah's life, but it was, at that moment, that time came to a screeching halt and then began again in an altogether different cadence. In slow motion and with agonizing hurt, Sarah remembered how it had happened. As usual, she had awakened early and gone into the kitchen to start breakfast. The letter had been placed in the cupboard, by the coffee container, so that Sarah would be the first to find it. Before she tore the envelope open, her mind already knew what her heart did not want to believe—Mary was gone. Her letter was brief. It said that she was leaving with Jason Carter. It went on to say that she loved her family, but there were things she had to discover for herself.

Mary had taken only a few personal things. The plain dresses, the head covering and sturdy shoes—all symbols of a lifestyle she no longer desired—were left behind.

Sarah had pleaded with Eli to try to find her, to bring her home, but she had been surprised at the swiftness and hardness of Eli's reaction. "I have only one daughter now," he pronounced. "Mary's name will not be spoken again in this home." And so, life went on as though she had not been. The community sanctioned his decision. Mary had chosen another way, and now she was no longer a part of them. There was no one for Sarah to talk to or share memories with. At first, Sarah had sensed that Eli was hurting, too, but he concealed it so well that, after a while, she questioned if he cared at all. This reaction of Eli's was a hard thing to understand. He was a good man. He had always been a good father and husband and so, because she knew that he was a good man and because it was their way, Sarah abided by the decision.

"Mamma,"

Sarah turned, startled. "Rachel, I didn't hear you drive up."

"James stopped at the barn. He wanted to talk to Papa," Rachel answered.

"Hello, Julie. I'm glad you've come to visit." Sarah said as she reached for her granddaughter. Julie raised her arms so that Sarah could take her. "Would you like some cookies and lemonade?" Sarah asked as Julie snuggled against her.

Julie looked at her grandmother with solemn eyes. Her face was flushed. Sarah felt the heat of Julie's body as she held her.

"She's still running a fever and has a strange cough," Rachel said, as she followed her mother into the kitchen.

"Why don't you take her to see Dr. Peter?" Sarah asked, as she thought of the thousands who were dying in Europe and the Middle East from a new, so far incurable, strain of a virus.

"I've been advised to take her to the clinic in Lancaster," Rachel replied.

"But I'd feel so much better about it if Dr. Peter could see her, Rachel. He's been our doctor for so long. You know he delivered all of you children, even though he isn't of our faith, I've always felt better knowing that he was a believer. I'll never forget his prayers before each of you were born, and his visits here to our home were such a comfort to Grandmother Stoltzfus during Grandfather Stoltzfus's long illness."

"Mamma, these are difficult times for all of us," Rachel explained, pointing toward the crops drying in the fields. "For four years in a row now we have had a drought, and it has taken its toll. We can't afford to keep the herd—the price of milk is down, and feed is just too expensive.

You all have the profit from the market, but James' family doesn't have that. James is here to see if Papa wants to buy some cows from our herd. James thought he'd give him the first chance at them."

Stunned, Sarah interrupted, "What will you do? The Zooks have always had the best dairy cows in the county."

"James can get a full-time job in town as a mechanic. He has a talent for fixing things.

We wouldn't sell the herd if we had any other choice," Rachel explained. "Look, it isn't just us. Many of our people are afraid. It isn't natural for us to be having so much trouble—with not enough rain year after year and the awful heat. There seem to be problems everywhere. Hannah Martin's sister wrote from Iowa, and they've had their crops destroyed by terrible storms and floods. Scientists have been warning everyone about global warming for many years. Since so many lives were lost during the coronavirus (COVID-19) pandemic, everyone is frightened and fearful of what is coming next. There is already a new, yet unidentified virus, spreading across Europe, Africa, and the Middle

East. We must do something before it becomes another pandemic. I agree with the politicians and religious leaders who believe that these disasters are God's judgments on the people of this world for their disobeying His commands and not caring about His creation. These leaders are calling for all nations and religions on earth to unite, with the purpose of making all mankind acknowledge God and obey His Word."

Rachel continued, "And it goes beyond natural disasters, besides worrying about the earth's overheating and how it is affecting all inhabitants, people in town are worried about the terrorist attacks that have happened in the cities with increasing frequency in the past few years. According to the militia, the anarchy is spreading, even to the countryside."

"We already obey God's commandments, and what is this talk from the militia?" Sarah asked. "Rachel, you know we don't listen to such rumors. Our trust is in God," Sarah cautioned.

"I know Mama," Rachel continued. "But the militias have greatly aided our government by keeping a close watch on possible troublemakers. I'm just saying that everyone is on edge. The Zooks and several others in the community agree with the national leaders that this is God's punishment on our country for not honoring Him.

Julie stirred in Sarah's arms. Sarah brushed the hair from the child's face and kissed her gently on the cheek, as she looked at her daughter. Like Tom, Rachel had inherited Eli's brown eyes and dark hair, but, at this moment, it was the set of her jaw and the determination on her face that reminded Sarah most of Eli.

"I understand how you feel," Sarah said softly. "Sometimes I think of the heat and the drought as a living thing that is determined to destroy us. I, too, wonder what is happening and how this is going to end, but I don't see why that has anything to do with Dr. Peter. I went to see him last week when I sprained my ankle, and he asked about all of the family."

Rachel's face reddened, "I know you saw him last week." It is time for us to go," she said abruptly, as she took Julie from Sarah's arms. """"I'm sorry if I've upset you, Rachel," Sarah said gently.

"I'm all right, Mamma. I'll let you know what the doctor says about Julie."

I wonder what is really troubling her, Sarah thought, as she watched Rachel walk down the lane to the barn.

Chapter Two

A Visit from the Brethren

"James, I know it has been a tough decision to make, but, under the circumstances, it's probably what you must do," Eli said to his son-in-law. "I'll see what I can do about buying some of the herd."

"Thank you, sir. It will be appreciated."

"We don't want charity," Rachel answered, as she approached the men.

"It isn't charity when it's for family," Eli responded. "Besides, it would be a pity to let the best milk cows in the county go to someone else. When you're in better circumstances, you can buy them back from me."

Julie squirmed in Rachel's arms, and James took her from Rachel.

"What's wrong with my granddaughter?" Eli asked, smiling at Julie.

A frown flickered across Rachel's face. "Her fever's come back," she said.

"We'd best be going and get her to bed," James replied. "Thanks, again."

"It's my pleasure," Eli said, placing his hand on James's shoulder. "Go in peace."

Dust swirled behind Rachel's and James's car, as they drove down the lane and out onto the county road.

"We need rain about as badly as I've ever seen," Eli said to Jonathan.

Another car slowed and turned into the Stoltzfus's driveway, as Eli and Jonathan started back into the barn. Sarah was in front of the house watering the few flowers that had survived the summer's heat, and she watched as the car stopped by the barn and John Lapp and Samuel Martin got out. *I wonder what that's about*, she thought, as she tilted her bucket and poured the last bit of water on the thirsty flowers.

"Well, you got here at just the right time," Eli greeted his brethren. "The chores are finished."

"Hello, preacher," Jonathan spoke politely to John Lapp and nodded to Deacon Samuel Martin. "I need to be going now," he said to Eli. "Amanda's expecting me."

"Stay if you can, Jonathan," the pastor said. "We'll only take a few moments of your time, and this is something that you need to know also."

"You're welcome to come up to the house and visit," Eli offered.

"No, we have others to see," Samuel answered. "We're here to let you know that there will be a meeting at the meetinghouse for tomorrow evening at seven."

Eli looked at his visitors. They'd been to his home dozens of times. John Lapp was a dairy farmer and their pastor. He, Samuel, and Eli had grown up together. Samuel nervously rubbed his chin and kept looking at John. John seemed ill at ease also.

"And why is the meeting being called?" Eli asked.

"You know that some within the congregation are experiencing difficulties," John said slowly.

Eli kicked at the dry soil. "We're all experiencing difficulties. Maybe you should invite a rainmaker to the meeting," he said, and then he smiled when he saw the surprised look on the pastor's face.

Samuel cleared his throat again. "It's more than that Eli. There have been problems with the town folks."

"What sort of problems?" Eli questioned.

"My nephew was in town yesterday, and a group of men approached him. They asked him if he was kin to the pastor. They accused our people of being the ones who are causing the troubles we're having around here."

"That's ridiculous," Eli stated. "Since when do we control the weather?"

"Hear us out," Samuel said, as he held up his hand. Then he added, "Some of our people have been told that they may lose their jobs if we don't…"

"If we don't what?" Jonathan asked.

"Go along with the mandates of the Concerned Citizen's Council," John answered, looking steadily at Eli. "Look, Eli, I'll get to the point. "One of the things they objected to was that several of our families have continued seeing Dr. Peter Graham, even after he has been censored."

Some of our people have been told that they may lose their jobs if we don't

Go along with the mandates of the Concerned Citizen's Council

"The Council?" Eli said, surprised. "I thought we hadn't joined the Council because we believe that the church and government should be kept separate."

"We've called the meeting so that the congregation can discuss it further. I understand how you feel, but unsettling events are happening. Rumors are spreading, causing people to react out of fear," the pastor explained.

"You'll come to the meeting, won't you?" Samuel asked.

"I'll be there," Eli stated.

After they left, Eli said goodbye to Jonathan and then stood looking at the house and fields beyond. The setting sun had left a rose-colored glow in the western sky. Near the horizon, the evening star hung bright and clear. In the distance, an owl hooted. Eli knew the woods where the owl's call had come from, just as he knew all of the land. He had been born in this place, and it was a part of him. He could close his eyes and still see the lay of it. The first Stoltzfus had settled here in the 1730s, as a part of William Penn's "holy experiment" of religious tolerance. The house that had been started by his great-grandfather was then finished by his grandfather. The two-story stone house was of solid construction, made to last, like the people who had built it.

Sarah had turned on a lamp in the front room, and light spilled out the door and shone behind the curtained windows. Eli could see her moving around inside, and he knew she was waiting for him, curious about the visit.

There was something else he must do first. He entered a side door of the barn. The door opened to a small room that served as an office. The familiar smells of hay, animals, and old wood surrounded him, and he was comforted by them. A handmade oak desk sat at one side of the room. Above it were shelves that held files where the business records of the dairy farm were kept. He walked to that side of the room and slid back a board in the wall.

Eli had discovered the safe there a long time ago, quite by accident. He had been adding some additional shelving when the board he was attaching suddenly popped open. There had been nothing inside the safe, which caused him to think that his great-grandfather had put the safe there and then died before he could use it.

He reached into the safe and pulled out two well-worn large books. The books had been part of a set called *The Bible Story* that he and Sarah had purchased years ago when the children were young. Because he'd had the same set when he was a child, he had wanted his family to have a set, but he had been unsure about the two religious books for adults that the salesman had shown him—he remembered that one was on church history and the other was a question-and-answer book. The man's name had been Paul Jordan, and Eli still remembered the earnestness he had as he presented the books. Later, Eli would conclude that he had bought the two large books because of that sincerity. Sarah had forgotten about the other two books when *The Bible Story* set arrived, and he had decided to read those books first before sharing them with her. In fact, he had thought about not reading them himself, but he had paid good money for those books and Eli Stoltzfus was not one to spend money on something he didn't use.

The book on church history was intriguing. He read with interest the section about Menno Simmons. The Mennonites had derived their name from Menno. For twenty-five years, Menno, his wife, and children had endured hardships and were often in peril for their lives as they spread the gospel in the Netherlands and northern Germany. Eli knew it was the desire to live in peace that had brought the Mennonites from the Netherlands to Pennsylvania. Other chapters in the book caused Eli to challenge what he was reading. That was when he began to value the other book that contained questions and answers. That book was full of the very questions he was beginning to ask.

All of the questions were answered with verses from the Bible. The text was provided, but he always checked it against his Bible. As hard as he tried, he could find no errors. He was fascinated by the prophecies in Daniel and Revelation and was convinced that earth's history was drawing to a close and that the Savior's return would be soon. The thing that puzzled him the most was the Bible teaching about the true Sabbath. The texts were clear about which day they should be observing, and he was amazed that his church could have been so deceived. Several times he started to share, with Sarah, the things he was learning. He also thought of presenting it to the congregation, but he was afraid that they would reject the idea and consider him a dissenter. If this happened, he knew the impact that it would have on their lives. He was Eli Stoltzfus, a Mennonite, and he could imagine no other way of life. He agonized for weeks and, finally, he decided that he would do nothing. He would not rob his family of their traditions and culture. He would not destroy the world that generations before him had built. And so, the books were put away, and he tried to convince himself that it didn't really matter. At night, when he lay awake struggling with his conscience, he thought of how much easier life would have been if he had never let Paul Jordan sell him those books.

A Visit from the Brethen | 19

Just when he thought he'd put it to rest, then the trouble with Mary had begun. Her questions had been hard ones, and he hadn't been sure how to respond. He had turned away from the truth, to preserve a way of life for his family. Then, his daughter—his youngest child and the joy of his and Sarah's life—had rejected what he had tried so hard to keep. He'd felt angry that she could so lightly regard what they held as sacred, but then he also felt guilty that he'd not had enough courage to address, openly, the questions she was now asking. Her questions had caused him to seek answers, and so he took out the books and studied them again.

Now, he placed the books beside his Bible on the desk and sat down. He needed time to think so that he would know what to do. He thought about the Concerned Citizen's Council. It had begun innocently enough in the 1990s as a grassroots organization of clergy and civic leaders intent on putting pressure on the public to elect and then demand moral accountability for those in public office. As new problems occurred throughout the world, the CCC became more powerful, until it had become the ultimate authority on moral and civil law. He slowly leafed through the pages of one of the books: *The Triumph of God's Love*. A sentence here, an underlined paragraph there, caught his attention and, as he read, switching from the book to his Bible and comparing texts, he became convinced that this time he must speak out. Dr. Peter Graham was being censored by the Concerned Citizen's Council because he was a keeper of the true Sabbath. This time, Eli would not keep silent. He could not let his people blindly become a part of causing good people to suffer.

When Sarah saw Eli leave the barn and start toward the house, she went to meet him. "Why did the Pastor and Samuel come by," she asked, not trying to hide her curiosity.

"A meeting has been called at the meetinghouse tomorrow night. It's about Dr. Peter. He's been censored by the Concerned Citizen's Council, and yet some of us are still seeing him," Eli said.

Sarah gasped, "Our church hasn't joined the Council. We wouldn't be a part of something that is so bent on enforcing religious laws through the power of government."

"I hope you are right," Eli replied.

Chapter Three

Church Meeting

Sarah stirred and opened her eyes, as a slight breeze disturbed the lace curtains at the bedroom window. She sat up, feeling for her slippers in the darkness. Her robe lay draped over the rocker where she had left it the night before, and she reached for it, pulling it around her. She walked to the window and gazed outside. A quiet stillness engulfed the land, broken only by the distant barking of a neighbor's dog.

She looked back into the room at the clock that sat on the dresser—the green digits glowed 4:00 a.m. She was an early riser, but she had awakened an hour earlier than usual. As she looked out the window again, she had an uneasy feeling that something had intruded into her sleep, startling her into consciousness. *Whatever it was it didn't bother Eli*, she thought to herself, as she listened to his steady breathing. The thought of crawling back into the comfort of the bed tempted her, but her practical side won. *I might as well get a start on the day*, she thought. She'd promised Eli that she'd help at the market that morning, and there were several other tasks that needed tending to before she left home.

Eli moved in the bed when a board squeaked as she crossed the room to pick up her reading glasses and Bible. He would have to get up soon enough, and Sarah didn't want to disturb him. She passed softly through the bedroom and went downstairs. Eli often teased her about being able to see in the dark—the way she could move around in the house without turning on a light. She smiled; she couldn't really see—at least not with her eyes—but, just as the land was a part of Eli, the house was a part of her. She and Eli had married young; she had been just seventeen and he nineteen, and this house had been her home ever since then. Eli was the youngest in his family, and his parents had insisted that they would move into the Grossdawdi Haus. The Grossdawdi Haus was a house built for aging parents, and it was attached to the side of the main house. This was an Amish and Mennonite custom. Although many of the younger generations of Mennonites preferred to live in their own homes, this custom had worked well for Sarah and Eli. Mamma Stoltzfus had been content making a home for herself and Dat Stoltzfus and had allowed Sarah the freedom she needed to make the big house her own. Sarah had enjoyed the friendship that flourished between her and Eli's mother, and she had been grateful for Mamma Stoltzfus's help and guidance, especially when the children were young. When Dat Stoltzfus had taken ill, Sarah knew that it was a comfort to Mamma Stoltzfus to have family nearby.

A pale gray had lightened the eastern sky, as Sarah settled into the overstuffed rocker in the front room. *What would this day bring?* she worried. She and God certainly had a lot to talk about, as she took her Bible and flipped on the lamp. She was concerned about the meeting at the church that night. The severity of the drought and the toll it was taking hit home when Rachel had informed her about their need to sell their herd. And there was Julie—Rachel would be taking her to the doctor this morning. Sarah smiled as she thought of her granddaughter, how quickly she had woven herself into their lives and hearts. Fear clutched her when she thought again of the virus that had killed thousands in Europe. Surely, something so deadly couldn't invade their quiet community. She had grown up feeling secure in her community and immune to the problems of the outside world. The Mennonites were God-fearing, hardworking and self-sufficient and, by tradition, they kept themselves apart.

A sound broke the silence. Sarah looked up. *Was someone outside?* she wondered. Her heart pounded.

Why am I being so fearful? she thought. *No one would….* Suddenly, a car engine roared and some glass shattered. The scream came from deep within her, "Eli, Eli!" She couldn't stop screaming, and then Eli was there. She felt the strength of his arms as he held her against him.

"Sarah, are you alright?"

"I think so. Someone was here. I heard a noise, and then the window shattered and…." They looked around. Shards of glass covered the floor. One piece lay on the arm of Sarah's chair.

"What's this?" Eli asked, as he bent to pick up a large object that lay on the floor amid the glass.

"Be careful," Sarah shuddered. "Maybe, it's a bomb."

"It's nothing so creative as that; it's just a rock covered in newspaper."

He carefully unwrapped the paper from the rock. A picture of Dr. Peter Graham in handcuffs dominated the front page. "Local Doctor Arrested," the headlines screamed.

"Who?" Eli questioned, as he walked to the door and looked out. The sky was becoming a soft blue. In the pale light, Eli could see the barn. He heard the cattle stirring. "I'd better check on the livestock," he said.

"The barn," Sarah gasped. "They didn't...."

"Everything looks normal from here. I need to get started with morning milking anyway," he answered.

"Be careful, Eli."

"It'll be alright, Sarah. They wouldn't hang around and, anyway, Jonathan will be here soon." He sat in the chair by the door and pulled on his boots. "I wonder where Rags and Little Bit are. It seems like we should have heard them barking."

Sarah shivered, as she remembered the feeling she'd had when she awoke. She'd sensed something was wrong. Had it been the dogs that awakened her? "I'll fix coffee and start breakfast," she said. "Ask Jonathan if he can join us."

She carried the newspaper with her as she walked to the kitchen. Dr. Peter being treated like a criminal—she couldn't believe it. All he'd ever done was help others and take a stand for what he believed was right. Wasn't that what America was all about—being free to follow your own beliefs? She thought back. Everything had changed since the terrorist attacks had begun a few years earlier. Laws had been changed to make it easier to catch these evil perpetrators. From military tribunals to the easing of restrictions on government censorship—the precedents had been set. Just when it seemed that the violence had been contained, other problems arose. Sarah sighed; fear and suspicion of everyone and everything had wedged its way into their lives and stayed like an uninvited guest.

Fear and suspicion of everyone and everything had wedged its way into their lives and stayed like an uninvited guest

Eli walked toward the barn. He paused and his jaw tightened as he saw the angry words the perpetrators had spray-painted on the front of the barn. His eyes scanned the scene. It was then he spotted the lifeless bodies of Rags and Little Bit sprawled in front of the barn entrance.

That was where Jonathan found him—kneeling beside the family pet—his hand stroking Rags head. "Papa, what's happened?" he asked quietly.

Eli did not move. "Jonathan, they shot the dogs to keep them from barking and trying to protect us."

He continued in a controlled, determined voice, "Always, I have tried to do what is right—for my family, for my friends. I have been a good neighbor. We are a peaceful people. We are to love our enemies. 'Whosoever strikes you on your right cheek, turn the other to him also.' It is what we have been taught to live by, and it has served us well." His back straightened and he stood.

"Papa, who is the enemy?"

"They are people who are angry because your Mother and I have not turned our backs on a good man," Eli said. He turned to face Jonathan and, looking into his eyes, he warned, "Worst things will happen before this is over."

"Should we call the authorities?" Jonathan asked.

"I suspect they already know," Eli stated.

Eli placed a tarp over Rags and Little Bit. "Sarah will want to see them before they are buried," Eli explained.

The inside of the barn had not been disturbed, and Eli and Jonathan went about the morning routine in silence; the gentle lowing of the cows and the swish-swish of the milking machine calmed them.

Business at the store was light that day. Although the Stoltzfuses had told no one, the news had traveled. Many of those who did come to shop avoided eye contact with Sarah, as she checked their purchases at the register. A few, making sure they were not overheard, told her and Eli they were sorry about what had happened

That evening, the meetinghouse was already packed when Eli and Sarah arrived. Eyes followed them as they walked to the front and took their customary seats. Sarah glanced across the aisle to where the Zooks sat. Rachael had stayed home with Julie. She had called to say that they wouldn't know the results of a series of tests that Julie had undergone for a couple of days.

Pastor Lapp walked to the podium and waited until the talking subsided. His discourse was brief and to the point, as he explained the reason for the meeting. Considering the perilous predicament of the community and the nation, the church needed to make sure they showed a cooperative spirit toward the organizations that were trying to help secure peace and safety for all.

"This is why I've asked Carlson Webb, the president of the local chapter of the CCC, to speak to us," the pastor concluded as he introduced Webb.

Eli observed the pastor. Eli thought, *He doesn't like this, but he's afraid to take a stand.*

"God's judgments are being brought on our country because of American's ungodliness," Webb began. "We must rid ourselves of those who refuse to obey the law and who, in so doing, are bringing hardships on all of us."

"Take the case of Dr. Peter Graham," he continued.

Eli quickly rose to his feet. "What about the case of Dr. Peter?" he questioned. "He has done us no harm. He simply wants to worship in the way he believes is right," Eli contended. "To avoid this kind of problem is why our church has always supported the separation of the church from the government, and it is why we should not become a member of the Council."

"Mr. Stoltzfus, I believe?" Webb replied with sarcasm. "First, the acts of terror in our country have been committed by religious men who were doing what they believed was right. Secondly, the constitutional provision for separation of church and state was to keep the church out of the administration of the government, not the other way around. The founding fathers never intended the state to become a godless government. The Council, with the cooperation of the Department of Homeland Defense, has adopted fair laws that will enable us to become one people, divinely led. By supporting the disobedience of one—in this case, Dr. Peter Graham—we are condoning all wrong acts. If your community of worshipers does not cooperate with the Council and join us in our pursuit of moral righteousness, you are committing anarchy, and we cannot protect you from the wrath of the citizens you are harming," he sneered.

> *If your community of worshipers does not cooperate with the Council and join us in our pursuit of moral righteousness, you are committing anarchy, and we cannot protect you from the wrath of the citizens you are harming*

Eli started to speak again, but was shouted down by several of his neighbors.

Sarah sat, looking straight ahead. Never had she imagined that such a spirit would pervade their church.

They're frightened, she thought, as she glanced at Rebecca Martin, who sitting in front of her. Rebecca held her youngest child tightly, as her husband rose to speak.

The debate continued. Each time an objection was voiced, Webb countered it with cleverly contrived answers and smooth words. Some of those listening were swept up by his charisma and shook their heads in agreement with his reasoning. Others listened quietly.

Finally, Eli rose and strode forward, "Have we so easily forgotten what we stand for and why our forefathers came to this country? For years in Europe, our people were persecuted. Thousands were martyred and thousands of others were driven from their homes by governments that tried to control the religious beliefs of its citizens. How can we now vote to become a member of this Council, which we all know is controlled by the United States government? It is this control that has put Dr. Graham in jail."

Those in the meeting shifted uncomfortably in their seats. "One other thing," Eli added. "We do not bear arms against anyone, friend or enemy. This is one of our fundamental beliefs, and so how can we possibly consider becoming a member of an organization that openly supports the militias?"

He turned to the congregation. "I can never, with a clear conscience, support the CCC," he said empathically. Then he turned and stalked out. A surprised Sarah rose and followed him down the aisle. A visibly shaken pastor stood with his hands outstretched. "As you can see Mr. Webb, we have some serious thinking and praying to do about this matter. I ask that you give us a week to discuss this, and then we will meet again."

"One week," Webb agreed.

Chapter Four

Troubles with Eli

Sarah slept fitfully. Images of the friends she'd grown-up with drifted through her dreams. She ran to greet them, but their faces became angry; each time she tried to get near, they drove her away.

Eli lay still all night, aware of Sarah's unrest. He wanted to reach out to her, but he had to have time to think. At times, he felt paralyzed, as if a heavy stone were crushing him. He arose early and went to the office. Darkness engulfed the land. A dog barked in the distance, and he thought of Rags and Little Bit. He felt as if he were in a dream. The Bible prophecies of end-time events that he'd studied and tried so hard to forget were unfolding before his very eyes. He had to get Sarah to understand—but what if she refused to listen? He couldn't imagine being without her support. How would he go on? Sarah mechanically fixed breakfast the next morning. She didn't know whether Eli had slept or not because when she had awakened, he was already up and gone from the house. She'd wanted to talk about the meeting on the way home, but he'd been quiet and withdrawn. His reaction had reminded her of the way he'd been when she'd tried to talk to him about Mary. She'd pleaded with him not to be so harsh—to listen with an understanding heart to their youngest daughter—but he'd been unyielding. She sensed then, as now, that there was something deeper that he wasn't saying. "If only he'd talk to me," she sighed.

"Trust in the Lord with all thine heart and lean not unto thine own understanding." The words came as clearly to Eli as though there was someone beside him speaking to him. That was the answer! It wasn't up to Eli Stoltzfus. He only had to admit his need, his weakness. He had to trust—not in himself—but in something bigger. He had to let go, but it was not his nature to do so. He was self-reliant. He took pride in being able to fix what was wrong, but this time he knew he did not have all the answers. He knew he might lose his family and friends if he turned his back on the traditions and beliefs that bound them together. He fell to his knees. The weight in his heart was crushing him—crushing him down into the earth, it seemed. Why was it so difficult to let go? To trust? "Oh God," he cried, "please help me." It was the cry that the heavenly Father longs to hear from each of his children. The cry of a human heart when it can no longer go it alone.

Suddenly, peace filled Eli's heart. A glow seemed to fill the office. The stoic Eli was whistling when Jonathan came to help with the milking. He wondered at the change he saw in his father, but he said nothing.

Later, Sarah noticed the spring in his step as he came into the house. Her heart leapt for joy! Could he have had a change of mind? As they sat for breakfast, he asked, "Isn't there a verse in the Bible that says for us to trust in Lord with all of our heart and to lean not on our own understanding?" Sarah was surprised, "Why, yes, Eli. I was reading it this morning. That verse is found in Proverbs 3:6. The next verse tells us to acknowledge Him in all our ways and that He will direct our paths."

Eli continued. "I felt comforted when I read that, as though it was God's message for me today." Eli looked at her intently. "You read that same verse this morning?"

"Yes," she replied.

He reached across the table and placed his calloused hand on hers. "It was a message for both of us."

There was an urgency in his voice as he spoke. "I must go to the market the first thing this morning and meet with Tom. I'm afraid that he is upset that my behavior is driving away customers. I'll be back before lunch and then we'll talk. I have something important to show you."

A line of picketers had formed in front of the market; they were bearing signs that encouraged shoppers to boycott the Stoltzfus's market and to trade at stores that were helping America by being members of the CCC. Eli drove his truck to the back entrance and entered through a delivery door. Tom met him with a ledger of accounts in his hand. "I hope your stance last night was worth ruining the business," he said curtly.

Sarah busied herself at home. Focusing on the tasks that needed attention was difficult with her mind wandering back to the conversation with Eli. What did he want to show her? If only he'd go along with whatever the congregation decided, maybe their lives would get back to normal.

She picked up the crumpled newspaper and read again the article about Dr. Peter's arrest. There had been no other news concerning him. She worried that he'd be considered an enemy of the nation and not be given a normal trial. She understood why Eli was upset about the good doctor, but their church's refusal to join with the CCC couldn't help Dr. Peter Graham now, she reasoned.

Eli arrived home earlier than expected. As they sat at the kitchen table, he placed his Bible and the two books he'd studied in front of her. "Do you remember these books?" he questioned.

Sarah frowned, "I don't think so."

"We bought them when we purchased *The Bible Story* set for the children," he explained.

Slowly he began to tell her of his hiding the books so that he could preview them before sharing them with the family. About how his reading of them had led him to study his Bible and, through his studying, he had begun to understand the books of Daniel and Revelations—and how the prophecies in those books of the Bible explained so many things that were happening in the world. He said how he had desperately wanted to tell her, but he'd not wanted to trouble her. He had been afraid that, if he shared this with the congregation, they would reject what he was showing them and shut him out.

"I put the books away and tried to quiet my thinking about the matter," he said. "I was doing it for you and the children, I told myself."

As he explained how the situation with Mary had brought all of this to his mind, he admitted how guilty he'd felt because he'd been afraid to take a stand for what he recognized as God's leading, Sarah began to understand why he'd dealt with Mary so harshly. A slow-burning anger, like spilled milk, began to spread through her. How could he have let his problems drive their daughter away? Then, as she looked at his drawn face and saw how his shoulders slumped against the chair, she began to realize the anguish he had been through.

"There is something more I want to tell you," Eli said. I know you have wondered why I'm so against us being involved with the CCC and why I've reacted so strongly to Dr. Graham's arrest," he continued.

"I think Dr. Graham's arrest is a terrible thing," she said. "But how could our congregation's not joining the CCC help him? We've always been a part of the church community, and it frightens me to think of not being there anymore. "

"I don't want that to happen either," Eli replied. "But Sarah, in my studying I discovered another thing--something very important." He hesitated, and Sarah looked at him puzzled.

"Have you ever wondered why Dr. Graham goes to church on Saturday instead of Sunday?" he asked.

"I suppose it's something about the Jewish law," she replied.

"It's not a law just for the Jews," he said. "It's in the heart of God's commandments. He asks us to remember the Sabbath day to keep it holy. According to the prophecies, at the end of earth's history, it will be a test of loyalty for His followers."

"Why, Eli, we go to church every Sunday," she exclaimed.

"The Bible says to remember the seventh day," he continued. "Sunday is the first day of the week. Saturday is the seventh day."

"But Jesus changed that when he was crucified and rose on the first day."

"I thought so too until I began to study. At first, I was convinced what I was reading was wrong. But it isn't an error. God didn't change his commandments. In Matthew, we're told that not one jot or title will be changed until all is fulfilled. God didn't change his law; mankind changed it. God says, 'If you love me, keep my Commandments.'—so they must be important."

"But then why does everyone go to church on Sunday, and does it really matter which day as long as we worship Him?" she asked, perplexed. "Besides, we are already Christians. We were baptized in the church when we were thirteen. We accepted Jesus as our Savior and asked forgiveness for our sins. Isn't that what is important?"

"It's the most important thing," Eli said slowly. "We committed then to let Him be in control of our lives. Remember the verse you read this morning about trusting the Lord and leaning not on our own understandings?"

How could their people for centuries worship on Sunday if it wasn't the Sabbath? His parents and hers had been godly people; they'd all studied their Bibles

"Yes," she replied.

"We have to trust Him and His Word—not just when it goes along with what we or others think—but in all circumstances."

"I know this is sudden, Sarah, but all that I'm asking is that we take time and study together," Eli pleaded.

She pushed away from the table and walked to the window. She wanted to distance herself from the things he was saying. He couldn't be right. How could their people for centuries worship on Sunday if it wasn't the Sabbath? His parents and hers had been godly people; they'd all studied their Bibles.

Wouldn't they have realized that they were worshiping on the wrong day?

The jangle of the telephone broke the silence that lay between them. Sarah reached for the receiver and answered.

"Mama," Rachael's voice quivered.

"Yes. Rachael, what's wrong?"

"Julie's a lot worse. We hope it is not the same virus that is affecting Europe. The doctor is meeting us at the hospital." She paused and her voice broke, "She is so sick, and I'm so afraid."

"I'm sure she'll be alright," Sarah said, pushing down the panic that threatened to engulf her.

"Your father and I will meet you there."

The drive seemed endless. A darkness filled Sarah's soul, a darkness that was as suffocating as the oppressing heat. She'd lost Mary. Was God going to take Julie, also? Didn't they have enough troubles without this happening?

Eli reached to comfort her, but she recoiled from his touch. Perhaps God was punishing them because of Eli's strange new beliefs. If only he'd forget these things he was telling her. But she recalled the intensity with which he'd shared the Scriptures, and she knew that he was determined.

Would she have to choose between Eli and her church family? The darkness inside her grew denser. "I am the light of the world." They'd studied that verse in the book of John during Bible class just a few Sundays ago. *Where was the Light now?* she wondered. The rest of the verse came to her, "He that followeth me shall not walk in darkness, but shall have the light of life." That's what she desperately needed—the light of life—for Julie and herself.

She remembered Julie wrapping her arms around her neck and how her brown eyes sparkled when she saw her grandparents. She thought of Rachael and James. How would they cope if they lost Julie? Sarah hurt for both her daughter and son-in-law. There had been such despair in Rachael's voice. If Julie's life was taken from them, could there be light in any of their lives?

The darkness inside Sarah seemed impenetrable.

They pulled into the hospital entrance and searched for a parking place. The lot was overflowing. There were people everywhere. Ambulance and police cars obstructed the emergency entrance.

"Eli, what's happening?" Sarah asked, alarmed.

"When I was at the market this morning, I heard that a lot of people had taken sick with something that sounded like what Julie has," Eli said. "Surely, that can't be what's wrong." "God help us," Sarah whispered.

Chapter Five

A Miracle for Julie

Eli and Sarah, hoping to avoid the crowds milling at the front of the hospital, rushed to a side entrance which they had often used when Dat Stoltzfus had been ill. An armed guard stopped them. Only authorized people can enter here," he said brusquely. "May I see your identity cards?"

Sarah looked at Eli; his face was expressionless. The national identity card had been another issue that their congregation had debated. At first, many—not only in their congregation, but in the nation—had been opposed to the "smart card," as some called it. But as the terrorist attacks worsened, while, at the same time, turmoil in Mexico and other Central American countries caused thousands to flood into the U.S. illegally, the pressure by the Homeland Defense Department to issue such a card became intense. Not only would the technology of the smart card curb the rise of terrorism, but it would also end the rising theft of credit and bank card numbers which had cost already financially strapped citizens millions of dollars. And so, the public had slowly been sold on the validity of the card.

The guard took their cards, inserted them into a small device he held in his hand and then flashed a light into Sarah's and then Eli's eyes. His expression softened as he said, "There is nothing on you. But, unless you have a family member who has already been admitted, you must go through the main entrance."

Eli started to explain, but then he saw James walking toward them.

"Rachael said you'd try this entrance," James said.

They followed James down the corridor to the elevators, where several people were waiting. "There are a lot of people who have taken sick with—whatever it is," he paused, his voice breaking. "I think my mother has the same illness."

"Has she been to a doctor?" Sarah asked.

"The doctor she usually sees is no longer available," he said stiffly.

"You mean Dr. Peter?" Eli said, his voice agitated. "We could all use him now."

James looked away without replying, and Sarah was relieved when the elevator door opened.

Julie had been placed in an isolation area of the children's ward, along with other children who had the same illness. They all paused in front of the large swinging doors. "We have to put on these before we enter," James explained, as he pointed to a stack of disposable smocks. "It's a precaution, so that the disease is not spread." They donned the smocks, caps, and shoe covers. As Sarah fitted the filter over her face, she worried that Julie would be frightened of them.

James pressed a button and the door was opened. Inside, a swarm of doctors, nurses, and technicians hurried between rooms.

Julie lay pale and small in the large bed. When she recognized her grandparents, a smile lightened her face for a moment. Rachael hovered by her side. Sarah went to Rachael and put her arms around her.

Rachael responded, but then pulled away.

Rachael has always been a good child, but her independent spirit has made it more difficult for me to get close to her, Sarah mused. *Even when she was little, though shy, she didn't want to be fussed over—didn't need or want anyone's help,* she remembered.

"The doctor said he'd be back in a while," James explained. "Maybe he'll tell us more then."

They sat waiting. Technicians and nurses came back and forth, drawing blood, checking vital signs. The clock moved slowly. Julie was sleeping when the doctor, along with several colleagues, entered. After glancing at Julie's chart, he wearily explained that, because they still had not been able to identify the cause of the illness, they were treating the symptoms. They were using several drugs, with the hope that one would be effective. Since the outbreak, doctors across the nation were working feverishly to come up with an answer—a treatment that would be effective—something that would give hope to both patients and families.

"I'm sorry," he said. "It's all we can do at this time."

The room felt cold, and Sarah shivered as they turned to leave.

"Are they saying our child is just a number, just one more case?" Rachel asked.

"Let's talk out in the hall for a moment," Eli said. Rachel hesitated but, seeing that Julie was now sleeping, she consented.

After some discussion, they all agreed that they had no choice but to trust that Julie was receiving the best treatment possible.

"Maybe it's a blessing that there are so many others," James said. "More people will be interested in finding a cure."

"Maybe so," Eli replied quietly.

Together, the family devised a plan for Julie's care while she was in the hospital. Rachel refused to leave Julie, but they decided that one other family member would stay with Rachel. Sarah would be the first.

"Before James and I leave, let's pray for Julie," Eli said.

They gathered around Julie's bed. Eli prayed fervently for Julie, their family, and for the others in the hospital. Sarah was surprised at the intensity of his prayer. Something had changed inside of Eli. After the prayer, Eli went to Julie's side, held her hand, and bent over and gently kissed her on the cheek. "God will be with you, Julie," he said softly.

The next few days merged into each other like an unending test of endurance. They settled into the new routine of being at the hospital, but, in spite of their hopes and prayers, each day they saw Julie growing weaker.

Newspaper headlines were filled with speculation about the cause of the disease that was beginning to kill so many. The government was accused of not doing enough. The CCC was blaming the community for not complying with the laws of God. The meeting at the church was postponed because so many in the congregation were sick.

Although he knew she was preoccupied and worried about Julie, Eli encouraged Sarah to study the things he had shown her. When she couldn't rest, Sarah found herself being drawn to her Bible and Eli's books. As she studied, she began to glimpse a vision of God and his purpose for the people of the earth. God had not ordained the dreadful events happening around her. It was mankind who had disobeyed God and forfeited eternal life. Because of their disobedience, evil had come upon the earth, and it was this same evil that still marred the perfect world God had created in the beginning.

She was intrigued by the prophecies in Daniel and Revelation that so accurately pinpointed the time in earth's history when the Messiah would come, give his life as a redemption for mankind, rise again, and return to heaven with the beautiful promise to come again for His people. She was equally fascinated as she read her Bible to discover that the prophecies foretold the events of nations, rulers, and the church—even until earth's final days.

Before Jesus returned to heaven, He promised His disciples He would send the Holy Spirit to be with them and to guide them into the truth. Now, Sarah felt His presence with her as she studied. Her world swirled around her, but, when she opened her Bible, a perfect calmness prevailed. The darkness that had oppressed her soul dissipated, and her mind became clear as she grasped the meaning of things she had never even considered.

One evening, Eli came home early from his stay at the hospital. "What's wrong?" Sarah asked, searching his face for a clue.

"Nothing's wrong," Eli replied seriously. "But I'm concerned about something that's happening. Have you heard of the Reverend Thomas Stone?"

"Isn't he that faith healer?"

"Yes, and he is a big supporter of the CCC and a friend of Carlson Webb. I suspect it was his urging that got Dr. Peter arrested."

"And how does this concern us?" Sarah asked.

"He's coming to the hospital—to heal the sick. The CCC has planned a big meeting," Eli paused.

"Rachel and James are excited; they think he can heal Julie, and Rachel wants us to be there."

Sarah gasped. A million thoughts swirled through her mind. Was it possible that this man was sent from God? "Actions speak louder than words." How often had she explained that simple fact to her children when conflicts arose. If that was the case, the Reverend Stone wasn't exactly to be admired, despite his claims to be a healer.

An agonizing discussion followed. Eli and Sarah could not possibly see how God's hand was in this. Eli looked up a verse in Matthew 24:4 about false prophets in the time of the end. At the same time, they both knew that, if they refused to be there, it would put a rift between them and Rachel. As badly as they wanted Julie to be healed, they felt uncomfortable with the idea of involving the Reverend Stone. After much thought, they reluctantly agreed to go and be with Rachel, James, and Julie.

The event was scheduled to happen the next morning. A large stage had been erected on the hospital grounds. Family members and friends of the ill would gather there for a dedication service before the Reverend Stone walked through the hospital wards, praying for the sick.

When Sarah awoke the next morning, dread filled her mind, and the awful darkness threatened to engulf her again.

Though the Stoltzfus family arrived early, crowds of people were already gathering at the hospital.

"You'd think the President was paying us a visit," Eli said, as he gazed at the entourage of cameramen, security personnel, and technicians setting up the equipment for the meeting.

"It looks as though all the major media networks are here," Sarah observed.

They went directly to Julie's room. Rachel greeted them excitedly, "I'm glad you came early.

They want everyone who can to attend the commitment ceremony."

"But what about Julie?" Sarah asked.

"The nurses say it will be alright to leave her, but..."

Eli interrupted, "Let your Mother stay with her. I'll go with you and James."

"Is that alright with you?" Rachel asked, relief showing on her face when Sarah nodded "yes."

As they left the room, Eli let the others go first, paused, and then briefly came back to Sarah. "God will protect us," he said softly.

Sarah had been surprised when Eli offered to go with Rachel because she knew how he felt about the Reverend Stone. Now she understood that he was trying to protect her.

Eli, Rachel, and James's footsteps echoed in the hospital corridors. There was an eerie quietness in the place, Eli thought. Outside, they were met by James's father and several other members of the Zook family. They wove through the hundreds of parked cars and even a few black buggies and patiently waiting horses that belonged to the more conservative, old-order Amish. As they paused to go through the security check, Tom and his wife, Katie, joined them. Eli noted that Jonathan and his wife, Amanda, had chosen to stay away.

It was only 8:30 in the morning, but the sun already blazed in the clear sky, and Eli wiped the perspiration from his forehead. They found a spot near a small tree and sat on the dry brittle grass. A choir and orchestra that had gathered on the stage began playing spiritual songs. The audience was invited to join the singing. Familiar hymns were gradually replaced by repetitive phrases, accompanied by loud, syncopated music. The onlookers swayed to the beat of the music as they repeated the verses, "Our God is wonderful; He is magnificent; His love is everything; He will send the Redeemer." Over and over, the phrases were repeated until the words blurred together in one giant, confusing barrage of noise. The sound rolled over them and, at its crescendo, the Reverend Stone—accompanied by Carlson Webb and other members of the CCC—came on stage. Webb stepped forward and welcomed the audience and the special guests, which included pastors who represented many of the churches in the area. Eli drew a long breath of relief when he saw that John Lapp was not among them—maybe there was hope yet.

"We are gathered here because of a crisis," Webb's melodious voice carried through the crowd. "Our friends and family are dying from a terrible disease. This disease was brought on our society because of our refusal to fulfill our moral responsibilities to our country and to God. Reverend Stone is here to offer forgiveness for our transgressions and to bring healing to our loved ones and our community."

Eli watched the rapt attention on Rachel and James's faces. Never had they been exposed to such emotion in their worship at the meetinghouse. He worried that the sensationalism of the moment would blind them so they could no longer see God's true leading in their lives.

Reverend Stone strode forward. Whereas Webb's voice had been like honey, smooth and harmonious, Stone's voice boomed from the podium like thunder. The power of his speech left everyone spellbound. His silver hair flowed back from his face in coiffured elegance. His dark suit and cuff-linked white shirt were impeccable. As he prayed, a shadow covered the sun, and Eli felt a chilling wind blow across his face. He glanced at his family, but they didn't seem to notice as they sat entranced. "Please God keep us in the hollow of your hand," Eli prayed fervently. After a lengthy prayer from Stone, the audience was instructed to stay and wait while he entered the hospital and visited each ward.

Julie slept most of the time now, her thin face flushed with the fever that ravished her body. She stirred in the bed and Sarah quickly bent over her. Suddenly, the room grew dark, pressing in on her. The hair on Sarah's neck rose as a coldness swept over her. "God, protect us," she prayed.

Still, in prayer, Sarah was not aware that the double doors of the ward had opened and that Stone and his staff now stood at Julie's door. Sarah jumped when she turned and saw them. Stone did not speak, but a brilliant light filled the room. The darkness had filled her, and now that light seemed so inviting, but, at the same time, Sarah wanted to run away for she sensed that it was evil. Stone walked on down the hallway, and the light faded from the room. Julie moved and opened her eyes, "Grandmother, I'm hungry," she said in a strong voice.

Chapter Six

A Family Gathering

"Push me again, Grandmother. I want to go really high," Julie's voice bubbled with enthusiasm. She stretched her legs out, throwing back her head, as the wind tugged at her dark curls. The rope swing had been made with a simple wooden seat, now polished smooth from years of use. It hung from a large limb of the old oak. Beneath the swing, the ground was packed hard from the feet of generations of Stoltzfus children, who had enjoyed that same simple pleasure. Sarah pushed and Julie laughed with delight as the swing rose and fell.

For the past few days, Eli and Sarah's emotions, like the swing, had swung from high to low. They were overwhelmed with joy when they saw that Julie was well, but then puzzled and unsure of what to make of Thomas Stone and Carlson Webb.

"One more time, and then we must go in and get ready for dinner," Sarah said, giving Julie one last push. Finally, the swing came to a halt, and Sarah took Julie's hand as they walked to the back door.

"Why is everyone coming here to eat? It's not even Sunday," Julie questioned.

Sarah smiled, "Well, your grandfather and I have something we want to share with the family before the meeting with Mr. Webb at the meetinghouse tomorrow night."

"Do you like Mr. Webb?" Julie asked. "Mother says he helped Reverend Stone make me well."

Sarah paused and looked down at her granddaughter. So many things had happened in the last few days. The country was abuzz with the news of the miraculous healings in Lancaster.

The Reverend Thomas Stone had mysteriously vanished and could not be found by reporters, but Carlson Webb's face was posted on social and news media sites, including YouTube, Facebook, Twitter, and every newspaper and television network in the country.

Julie, seeing the serious expression on Sarah's face, asked, "Grandmother, aren't you happy that I'm well? I was so very sick, and Mama said that everyone was sad. Were you sad?"

Sarah stooped down and gathered the small child in her arms. "I was very sad when you were sick, and I'm really happy that you are well. I love you so much, Julie," Sarah said, giving her granddaughter a hug, as she planted a kiss on her forehead.

Julie's arms tightened around Sarah. "I love you, too—but Grandmother do you like Mr. Webb and Reverend Stone?"

Sarah sat down on the top step of the porch with Julie beside her. "You are full of questions today, aren't you? First, I believe Jesus made you well without the help of the Reverend Stone or Mr. Webb. Second, Jesus wants us to love everyone, even our enemies."

"Now, we've got work to do, young lady," Sarah said, getting up before Julie could ask anything more.

A barrage of savory smells greeted them as they stepped into the kitchen. Sarah checked the roast chicken and bread stuffing baking in the oven and eyed the cherry pies sitting on the countertop. Then she kept Julie busy placing the flatware by the plates at the table while she made last-minute preparations for the meal. At last, everything was ready, and they sat on the front porch waiting for the family to arrive.

Eli drove slowly from the market, but instead of taking the usual route, he turned on a narrow gravel road that ended at a knoll overlooking the surrounding countryside. Stopping the truck, he walked to a rock outcropping and sat in the shade of one of the three large hemlocks growing there. As a youngster, they had come here to pick the blackberries that hung thick and juicy on the tangled brambles growing near the rocks. His mouth watered as he remembered the crusty cobblers Mother Stoltzfus had made from those berries.

Later, as a young man, he found this spot to be a place of solace and respite. Here, more than anywhere else, he felt connected to the land.

> *The Reverend Thomas Stone had mysteriously vanished and could not be found by reporters, but Carlson Webb's face was posted on social and news media sites*

He had come here when Dat Stoltzfus lay dying and, then renewed, he had gone back to the farm to comfort his mother and family. He'd come here again at his mother's death and when Mary left. It was his place of comfort.

The land stretched below him, with the now-dusty brown of the dry fields, interrupted by dark green where the trees grew near the creeks and field boundaries, and the thin ribbons of road that crisscrossed the countryside. The Stoltzfus farm was nearest and he thought of the family gathering that was planned for tonight.

They'd all be there, wondering what the occasion was to be invited to gather on a workday. They'd sit at the table together: Tom and Katie, Jonathan and Amanda, Rachael and James, and now Julie, too—only one would be missing. He yearned to see his youngest daughter, to explain to her the wonderful message he had discovered in God's Word. He wanted her to know that the world was standing on the brink of eternity and that soon Jesus would return. Was she still a believer or had his harshness turned her away forever? How would she make it through the tumultuous times ahead without God's light to guide her? What about the rest of the family? Somehow, he must make them understand. The decision that faced all of them was simple but crucial—choose to obey God or choose to follow man. This decision would ultimately seal their fates. It was the same decision that would face all the earth's inhabitants. Could Sarah and he be faithful, if, after tonight, there were other empty spaces at the table?

With a heavy heart, Eli knelt to pray. "God, please help me tonight to be your vessel. Help my family to see your love and purpose for mankind and help them to choose your Word above all else. Rescue them from the deceit around them, and give Sarah and me the strength to do your will. Amen." Then with a lightened heart, he arose, ready to greet his family.

As the late afternoon sun cast long shadows across the fields, the family members began to arrive. A few high, wispy cirrus clouds stretched across the dome of the sky, and a gusty wind began to blow, bringing some relief from the stifling heat of the day.

"Mama, you've cooked a feast and, on a Thursday," Rachel exclaimed, as she entered the kitchen.

"I helped Grandmother; I helped fix it all," Julie bounded into her mother's arms.

"I'm glad to know that you're a good helper," Rachel replied, giving her daughter a hug.

"I hope she wasn't a bother."

"She's a joy to have around," Sarah replied.

"Come in Amanda and Katie," Sarah greeted her daughters-in-law. "Jonathan told us the good news this morning. Rachel, Julie's going to have a cousin."

"Amanda, you're expecting!" Rachel and Katie responded in unison. The next moments were spent in happy chatter as the women put the food on the table.

Eli and the boys came in from the barn. They gathered at the long table and, before they ate, they bowed their heads, as Eli offered a blessing on the food and those around the table.

Sarah sent up a fervent plea to God as Eli prayed. She, too, was unsure of what their children's reactions would be to Eli's and her decision.

She looked down the table at her family. She was proud of each of them. They had grown into responsible adults who upheld well the traditions they had been taught. She felt the familiar ache of sadness when she thought of Mary. Tonight, other's fates could also hang in the balance, and she willed herself not to think of the one who was already missing.

As they enjoyed the meal, the fiery sun sank behind a low bank of dark clouds in the western sky. Slowly, the stars began to light up the evening sky, but the menacing clouds spread quickly, blotting out each twinkling light.

They finished the meal; Sarah and Rachel cleared the table and served the cherry pie. Then Eli spoke, "I know you're wondering why we've asked you to come tonight. Thank you for being too polite to ask." They laughed nervously. "There are things your mother and I want to share with you. You know we are living in very troublesome times."

He paused and looked down the table at each of them. "I only wish that Mary were here, for I am afraid that my refusal to listen to her—my harshness with her and my unwillingness to answer her questions —drove her from us." Sarah saw the surprise on their children's faces, for it was the first time their father had mentioned their sister since she'd left three years earlier.

Eli continued, "I dealt harshly with Mary because I felt guilt for concealing from Sarah, from you, and from my fellow believers the truth I had found in God's Word."

With an edge to his voice, Tom asked, "What truth?"

Then Eli began to earnestly share with them, as he had with Sarah They listened politely and, when he had finished, Amanda, her brown eyes gleaming, spoke. "I already know about the things you are saying. When I was small, I spent a good bit of time with my grandmother. Sometimes she would bring out a large book. It was a question-and-answer book like you say you have, Papa Stoltzfus. I loved the picture of Jesus coming again. Grandmother said that was her favorite, too. She also told me that one day we would all worship on Saturday, instead of Sunday, because it was God's true Sabbath."

"Well, I always saw her at the church on Sunday," Tom retorted.

"What Amanda is saying is true," Jonathan interjected. "Her grandmother left her the book."

"Grandmother went to church on Sunday, because I don't think she knew what else to do," Amanda continued. "But I remember she always got her work done on Friday. When grandfather would ask her about why she worked so hard on the day before the preparation day, she'd reply that Saturday was her special day."

"So, what does this all mean?" Rachel asked.

"It means, Rachel, that your father and I will keep the Sabbath on the seventh day, and the store will be closed on Saturdays," Sarah said.

It means tomorrow night at the meetinghouse I will again try to persuade the brethren not to join the CCC, and I will show them—to the best of my ability—what I have learned from the Scriptures," Eli concluded.

"Tell me," Rachel questioned, indignant at the mention of the CCC, "If the CCC, Carlson Webb, and the Reverend Stone are so evil, how could they have healed Julie?"

"God will have to judge Carlson Webb and the Reverend Stone," Eli replied quietly. "All I know is that God asks us to love Him and to keep His commandments. According to the Scripture, in the last days, God's test of loyalty for his people will be whether they keep His law and have His testimony in their hearts. I hope all of us will pass that test," he finished.

Sarah interrupted, "Your father explained to me that, down through history, there has always been a group of people who obeyed and cherished God's Word—even though the rest of the world laughed and tried to destroy them."

"A remnant is what the Bible calls them. They are the ones who remain faithful to God before our Lord's return," Eli said.

Tom pushed away from the table, "I've never heard anything so ridiculous. You mean you will risk ruining the family business. If you close the market on Saturday, you will be censored in the same way as your Dr. Graham."

"Maybe even put in jail," Rachel added. "I can't think of how awful it would be for all of us. Who would have believed that my parents would turn against all they have taught us?"

"Not all that we have taught you," Sarah added. "We have always taught you to love God, but the mistake your father and I made was to teach you to trust, without question, the traditions of the congregation and our forefathers."

Just as a heated debate began, blinding streaks of lightning flashed across the angry sky, the lights flickered, and a wind-driven sheet of rain and hail slashed against the side of the farmhouse. A mad scramble to close windows and doors ensued. Eli lit the oil lamps which sat on the mantle in the living room, and they gathered in that room as the electric lights flickered again and then stayed out. The steady roar of thunder and the pounding hail and rain throttled any attempts at normal conversation. Apprehension filled the air, as they waited for the violent storm to subside. "Let's pray for God's protection," Eli suggested, and they politely bowed their heads in prayer. As Eli prayed, a bolt of lightning tore through the sky. An ear-splitting boom and a blinding ball of fire lit the darkness, as the bolt found its mark; the ancient oak where, only a few hours earlier, Julie had been swinging, split apart.

Finally, the storm subsided, and the family members—as split in their thinking as the oak—and anxious to see if damage had been done to their homes, bid their parents good-bye and drove away.

Chapter Seven

Decision

The next morning, the blazing sun rose on a world still reeling from the storm of the previous night. The wind had toppled trees onto power lines, and the power was out over a large portion of the county. The electricity came on about three o'clock at the Stoltzfus home, saving Eli the trouble of starting the generator so that the cows could be milked.

Coming in from the milking, he found Sarah standing on the back porch, gazing at the splintered oak. The rope swing lay crumpled in the dirt, half hidden under a fallen limb.

"A penny for your thoughts," Eli said as he came up and put his arm around her.

"I was thinking about how quickly our lives can change. One moment it seems that things will always go on the way they have. Yesterday, Julie was swinging from the rope swing—the same way that her mother and you did before her. A swing has hung from the same limb of that old oak for generations. Sarah brushed away a tear, "I know I'm being silly, but I feel such a loss."

"I understand," Eli said, looking out over the battered fields of brown corn. "There is one thing we can be thankful for. The hail didn't ruin our crops. We'd already lost them."

Sarah smiled, "I guess you're right."

Eli replied, "What I fear most is the storm that is coming tonight at the meetinghouse. If the congregation rejects what I share with them, you do understand what it will mean for us."

"I understand," Sarah said softly.

"Tom stopped by the market last night to check on damage and there was none, but I need to go in early today. I'll post some notices so that shoppers will know that we'll be closed tomorrow." Sarah squeezed his hand, "I'll be praying for you."

Customers who stopped at the Stoltzfus Market were surprised to see neatly lettered signs announcing that, from now on, the market would be closed on Saturdays. Some were curious as to why this was, and Eli was able to share his love for God's Word with those who would listen. Others became angry and left. Most were simply afraid and made a note not to shop at the market again for fear that the CCC would brand them as troublemakers. Since using the smart card for all transactions was mandatory, it was a simple thing for the government to check the spending habits of anyone whom they considered suspect.

On that Friday, the people of the county had much more to be concerned about than worrying worry about whether the Stoltzfus Market would be open the next day. The storm had gained in intensity as it swept across the area, and communities to the east had suffered a great deal of devastation. Homes had been destroyed, and many were injured. Three deaths had been reported. For the first time since the healings in Lancaster, Carlson Webb was not mentioned in the news reports.

> *The people of the county had much more to be concerned about than worrying worry about whether the Stoltzfus Market would be open the next day*

In the same news reports that contained videos of storm damage, reports of injuries, and survival stories, a small story aired, which had been taken from one of the national news services. It said that reliable sources were accusing the government of covering up data taken from the latest technology that had been designed to spot uncatalogued, earth-threatening asteroids and comets. Supposedly, a newly discovered asteroid was hurdling on a direct collision course with planet earth. The government denied the accusations, but now two astronomers from Russia were confirming the discovery.

That afternoon Rachel Zook put Julie down for a nap and then walked the path to their mailbox. She was troubled about the strange ideas her parents were obsessing about. Although James was adamant about their not having anything to do with these teachings of Eli and Sarah, a desire to listen to her parents would not be quieted. Her feelings swung from one extreme to the other; she was angry with her parents for putting her in this position, upset with James for demanding that she not have anything to do with her parents' ideas, and frustrated with herself for not knowing how to handle the situation—not to mention embarrassed at what her friends were going to think.

Rachel, deep in thought, put her hand into the mailbox and pulled out a white envelope with scrawled handwriting. Without even reading the return address, she immediately knew who the letter was from. She hurried to the kitchen, sat at the table, and tore open the envelope. The letter began in Mary's usual enthusiastic, bubbly style. She described in detail a picnic she and Jason had gone on in the mountains just west of their Boulder, Colorado, apartment. She mentioned the shop where she worked, asked about Julie and the rest of the family, and—as always—she wanted to hear some news about her parents.

Rachel paused, thinking back. The first letter, with a Denver postmark but no return address, had arrived about six months after Mary had left. Rachel wondered if she should share the news with Sarah, but Mary had pleaded with her not to tell. Three months later another letter arrived, this time with a return address written inside, and so their correspondence began. Rachel did not understand how Mary could leave her family and their lifestyle. Her leaving had hurt Rachel deeply, because—being the older sister—she had always felt responsible for Mary. So, even though her father forbade them to speak of her, Rachel had rationalized that keeping in touch with Mary was her duty and that, perhaps, it was a means of bringing her wayward sister back to the family.

She had been shocked when her father mentioned Mary last night and surprised that he'd blamed himself for her leaving. When Mary left, Rachel had accepted Eli's reaction as justification for the shame that Mary had caused her family. Rachel noticed her mother's silence and, although Sarah tried to conceal it, there was a sadness about her that had not been there before.

Rachel sometimes wondered how Sarah would have reacted if she had left.

She looked down at the letter and continued reading. "The most wonderful thing has happened," Mary wrote. "Two young girls came by our apartment selling some magazine-like books. One looked just like *The Bible Story* books we had as children. I bought one because it made me think of home."

Just then, Julie whimpered and Rachel, the letter in her hand, got up and went to check on her. The child had fallen back into a deep slumber and, for a moment, Rachel sat on the bed and watched her sleep. Her heart overflowed with gladness when she thought of how Julie had been healed. When she looked at her daughter, she could not understand how her parents were so convinced that Carlson Webb and Reverend Stone were wrong. Lying down beside Julie, Rachel continued reading. "The girls offered to study the Bible with us. Jason wasn't raised in a Christian home, so he didn't know much about the Bible, and you know that I had questions about our beliefs. The studies have been fascinating. Rachel, did you know the Bible teaches that we are living at the very time when Jesus will come again? And another most interesting thing—we found out that these girls worship on Saturday, the seventh day of the week, just like Dr. Peter did. We have discovered God never told us to worship on the first day of the week. God didn't change His commandments, people did."

Rachel stared at Mary's words in amazement. How could her sister who lived so far away be caught up in the same religious belief as Eli and Sarah? The words blurred as Rachel read on. Mary explained why she and Jason now believed they should worship on Saturday. Mary ended the letter by saying that they were going to be baptized and then married very soon. She said, "I only wish that I could tell Mama and Papa how happy I am. I want them to know how much Jason and I love each other and how Jesus has become our best friend.

Rachel's confused thoughts were interrupted as Julie stirred, opened her eyes, and looked at her mother, "What's wrong Mama?"

Rachel looked at Julie, placed the letter in her pocket, and reached over to pick up her daughter. "Oh, nothing," she said.

This time, Eli and Sarah arrived early at the meetinghouse. Pastor John Lapp was in the back, and Eli went to talk with him. Sarah looked at the familiar worship room. She had been coming here since she was a baby. It was here that she had first noticed how handsome Eli Stoltzfus was and had blushed when he caught her gazing at him. The church was as much a part of their lives as was their home. She pushed away her anxiety as she thought of never worshiping here again. An even greater concern was that her church family would not accept God's message for these last days and that they would not be prepared for what lay ahead. So much hung in the balance tonight.

The church filled quickly. Amanda and Jonathan came and sat by Sarah. Tom and Katie sat several rows behind them and barely nodded when Sarah turned to greet them. James took a seat with his family and did not look toward the Stoltzfus family. Rachel had chosen to stay home with Julie. Eli had not come back to their seats, and Sarah looked around, puzzled, as John Lapp rose to greet the audience.

"We have come here to make a serious decision that will affect us all," Pastor Lapp began. "I have decided to let one of our own members speak first, Brother Stoltzfus, will you share with us what you have been telling me," he added as Eli, his Bible in his hand, strode down the center aisle.

Eli stood behind the podium and looked over the audience. "The last time we met, I begged us not to join the CCC because it is so closely connected to the government. The CCC has already coerced, censored, and arrested citizens who chose to worship in a way not recommended by our government. I reminded you that our belief that the government and the church should be separate is our Christian heritage. Persecution, because of our religious beliefs, is why our forefathers came to this country. This nation was a place where we and every citizen could be truly free to worship or not, as we—not the government—felt was right."

"Now," Eli continued, as he held up his Bible, "I want to explain why it so important at this time for each of us to have that same freedom— the freedom to worship as we choose without the government telling us differently. I want you to understand why it is urgent for each of you to take this Book and study the Scriptures to find out what God's message is for the time in which we are living."

There was murmuring in the congregation, and a man whom Eli did not recognize spoke out, "Does this have anything to do with your not opening the market tomorrow?"

"It does," Eli answered. And then, with conviction, he began to explain the Scriptures and the message in them that had led him to his decision. The people listened for a while, but what they were hearing was too much for them to accept. One man accused Eli, "You talked about our forefathers, but now you are saying their beliefs were wrong,"

"They lived according to the truth that God revealed to them," Eli tried to explain, but others interrupted.

James Zook's father addressed Eli, "Carlson Webb and the CCC brought Reverend Stone to us. He healed me and your own granddaughter. My wife and many others, who were on the verge of death, are here tonight because of them. How can you say that they are evil?"

"The Bible plainly tells us that there will be those who perform miracles in God's name who are not righteous. We are also warned that, in the last days, false prophets will appear and perform great signs and miracles to deceive even the elect," Eli answered. Then he started to provide Bible texts to back up his statement.

But before he could say more, Carlson Webb came forward. "I think it is time I defend myself. As you can see, Mr. Stoltzfus obviously has a grudge against me; perhaps he wishes it had been he who healed his granddaughter instead of the Reverend Stone. Perhaps then it would be easier for you to believe that he is right and that I am evil." Then Webb put his index fingers to each side of his head like horns and made a ridiculous, evil expression with his face.

The audience laughed, and one man yelled at Eli, "Your granddaughter was healed by Stone, but where is a sign from you, Brother Stoltzfus? A sign so that we will know whom to believe."

"Perhaps the person who asked that question should read what our Savior said in Matthew 12:39," Eli answered.

Several people in the congregation reached for their Bibles and began looking for the text. Shy Rebecca Martin stood and began to read the text aloud, "An evil and adulterous generation seeketh after a sign; and there shall no sign...."

"The text is being taken out of context," Carlson Webb interjected in a shrill voice.

The congregation turned to those seated next to them and began heated discussions. During the commotion, Eli—feeling he had said enough and seeing the mood of his fellow believers—slipped off the platform and out the side door. Sarah, seeing Eli leave, quickly followed him out the door. They got into the truck and drove the short distance to home.

Later, they stood in their backyard in the quiet stillness of the night. The barred owl hooted from the woods at the edge of the cornfield and myriads of stars shone like beacons in the dark sky. "I guess it didn't go so well," Sarah said softly. "What will we do now?"

Eli, looking into the heavens, replied, "We'll depend on the Creator of all of this. We'll live from day to day, and His Word will guide and sustain us."

The next morning as she arose to make breakfast, Sarah felt the difference, though subtle, in the weather. The day was dawning bright and clear, but the oppressive humidity had lifted, and a gentle breeze fluttered the kitchen curtains. "Perhaps we'll have an early fall," she said to Eli when he came in from milking.

Eli nodded, "Maybe so. Then he added, "I was talking with Jonathan while we were milking, and Amanda and he want to come over today and study the Bible with us. Amanda wants us to see her grandmother's book."

"Oh, that's wonderful!" Sarah exclaimed. "I was wondering how we'd spend this day. It seems that we should be at church, but I don't see how that's possible."

"It's a nice day, perhaps we could have a picnic," Eli added.

"A picnic—I like the idea. Where would we go?"

"I was thinking about the knoll where I used to go to pick berries when I was a child," Eli replied.

"I'll call Amanda and make plans," Sarah answered. "Do you think we should invite Katie and Tom?"

"Tom is still seething about my closing the market on Saturday. I think it would be better to give him some time to settle his thinking, as the market seems to be the only thing that is important to him right now," Eli said rubbing his chin. "I'm not sure about Rachel. She didn't come to the meeting last night. I guess you could ask, but I know that Julie would like a picnic."

Sarah went immediately to call Rachel. James answered and, when Sarah asked to speak to her daughter, there was a pause. Then, James, very coldly, said that Rachel was busy.

Later, as Jonathan and Amanda met them for the picnic, they drove to Eli's spot. Amanda brought the book her grandmother had treasured. The book had been carefully wrapped in a linen cloth and kept in a specially constructed cedar box. The pages were yellowed with time, but Grandmother's handwritten side notes and underlined sentences had not faded. After comparing the book with Eli's, they found that they were the same, only Amanda's was a much older edition. They began their study by reading Grandmother's notes and comparing them with verses from their Bibles.

The couples sat in the shade of the hemlocks, engrossed in the passages of Scripture they were reading. Birds sang and fluttered from limb to limb. A squirrel fussed noisily at the four intruders who were sitting under his tree. Everyone's senses were uplifted by the change in temperature and the pastoral scene that spread below them.

The sun climbed higher in the sky and then began its descent when, looking at the two baskets of food the women had brought, Jonathan declared, "I believe its past my lunchtime."

Sarah looked up, startled, "My, where has the time gone?"

The crusty homemade bread, roasted chicken, and apple pie that Amanda and Sarah had quickly packed were soon gone, and they sat together, contentedly, enjoying the peaceful moment.

After a while, Eli pulled from his pocket, a handwritten note. "I think there are others in our congregation who believe as we do. Pastor Lapp seemed interested in what I was saying and, last night as I was leaving the meetinghouse, Samuel Martin, stuffed this into my pocket."

They looked at the hurriedly written note. The short message read, "Thank you for standing for what is right."

"Sarah, how would you like to go with me to visit the Martin's? They may need our encouragement."

"I'd enjoy seeing Hannah," Sarah answered. "I have a dress pattern of hers I need to return."

"We need to pray for all of our people that they will have the courage to follow their convictions," Eli said.

"Including Rachel, Tom, and their families," Sarah added.

"We all need encouragement," Amanda said looking at Eli and Sarah. "This time of studying together has meant so much to me."

"It's meant a lot to all of us," Sarah said, putting her arms around Amanda. "I'm pleased that you and Jonathan are having a child. I fear the announcement about the expected little one lost some of its impact with Eli's revelation to everyone and then the storm."

"Jonathan and I understand," Amanda said, her face beaming.

The following day, Rachel Zook and Tom Stoltzfus attended services at the meetinghouse for the first time without either of their parents being there. Some members came to them and told them that they were sorry about Eli and Sarah. Some had questions. Others simply avoided the issue, speaking to both as though nothing was unusual.

Julie was puzzled and kept begging for Grandmother and Grandfather. During a break in the services, Rachel decided to take her outside where she could try to explain to her why her beloved grandparents were not at church. With Julie in tow, she darted out the side door just in time to hear two members discussing the Stoltzfus situation. "Well, I guess we can understand now why Mary left.

An apple doesn't fall far from the tree," said one.

"I never thought of it that way, but you're probably right," said the other.

They looked up, startled to see Rachel. Rachel, her face burning, rushed past them pretending not to have heard.

After church, Mrs. Zook invited Rachel and James to come to their house for Sunday dinner.

"Thank you for the invitation, but we need to go home today," Rachel spoke before James could reply. "Julie is fussy and I'm not feeling well."

On the way home, Rachel explained to James, "Your parents were having others over from the congregation, and I just couldn't face any more condescending looks or questions."

Chapter Eight

A Warning

The Concerned Citizen's Council wasted no time sending a warning to Eli. The registered letter arrived on Tuesday. Sarah's heart pounded, as she watched Eli open the official-looking envelope.

The message was short and to the point. "Since the Stoltzfus Market provides a necessary service to the community, being closing on Saturday—the preparation day for the Sunday Sabbath—would cause a hardship for the citizens of the community. If the market is not kept open this following Saturday, Eli Stoltzfus will be censored." In bold type the mandate continued, "To be censored means that all requirements stipulated by the CCC must be met within a week or the person being censored will face a hefty fine and possible arrest."

Sarah sat dazed as the reality of the situation hit. They'd known that this could happen if they closed the store. It was certain that Carlson Webb wouldn't miss a chance to pay Eli back for his open opposition to the CCC.

> *It was certain that Carlson Webb wouldn't miss a chance to pay Eli back for his open opposition to the CCC*

A thousand thoughts flashed through her mind. How big of a fine would they be required to pay? And if they still refused to submit would they lose their home? The market? No wonder Tom was so upset. Eli's forefathers had built the house and started the market. Eli and she were caretakers of these things. They had been faithful and improved what had been given to them, but did they have a right to forfeit their children's inheritance?

Darkness again filled Sarah's soul. Her heart ached with the thoughts of Tom and Rachel's rejection. Rachel still refused to speak with them, and they hadn't seen her or Julie since the night they had met with the family. Sarah wanted to escape, to run away from the terrible happenings that were wringing all hope from her heart.

Eli, the notice in his hand, paced the floor. His mind raced. What should they do? They could leave for a while, but where would they go? Absorbed in his own thoughts, he did not think of Sarah until he saw her go out the back door.

He found her sitting by the creek that ran through the back of their property. "Sarah," he said softly. She turned her tear-streaked face toward him and, when he looked into her eyes, he saw her desperation. Sobs racked her body as he held her in his arms. "It's too much; I can't bear anymore," she moaned. "We're losing Tom and Rachel; they'll have nothing to do with us and, now, if we don't agree with the CCC, you'll be put you in jail, just like Dr. Peter.

They stood holding onto each other—two people alone, awash in a tide of events that threatened to destroy them. Slowly, the words of a psalm that Eli had memorized for a school program when he was a child began to form in his mind, and he began to repeat the familiar verses from Psalms 91:1–4. "He that dwells in the secret place of the Most High shall abide under the shadow of the Almighty. I will say of the Lord, He is my refuge and my fortress: my God; in Him will I trust."

Sarah looked into his face, hesitated, and then blended her voice with his. In unison, they repeated the next verses, "Surely, he shall deliver thee from the snare of the fowler and from the noisome pestilence. He shall cover thee with His feathers and under His wings shall thou trust; His truth shall be thy shield and buckler."

"God will supply the answers," Eli said. "We must remember to trust Him."

"We must," Sarah agreed. The darkness lifted, and the light of God's love filled her heart.

Tuesday afternoon, Rachel Stoltzfus made a decision. She could not go against the wishes of her husband; she would not defy the teachings of her church. She'd suffered enough already with the embarrassment of it all—with her parents dishonoring their heritage. When she thought of how her decision would hurt her mother and father, she put aside the guilt she felt and decided it was their fault. They had brought this on themselves. After thinking about it for a while, she decided that there would be one last thing she would do for her mother—she would give her back Mary.

Leaving Julie with James, she drove the familiar route to the Stoltzfus farm and, making sure no one saw her, she quickly left Mary's letter in the mailbox. Then, turning her back, she headed home to James and Julie. When she arrived, James handed her the newspaper. A picture of Reverend Stone walking among the sick in a hospital filled the front page. The headline said, "The United States Sends a Savior to Europe." Rachel read it, and—although she smiled—a coldness filled her heart.

Chapter Nine

The Letter

The next morning, Sarah noticed that the mailbox had been left partially open. Thinking that Eli had forgotten to shut it the day before, she absent-mindedly slowed the car, rolled the window down, and reached out to shut the mailbox when she saw a white envelope inside.

Eli left some of the mail yesterday, she thought, as she reached inside the box.

Puzzled she held the crumpled envelope, with the somehow familiar writing, in her hand. She saw that it had been opened and then taped shut again. "This is addressed to Rachel—why was it delivered here?" she questioned. In the left-hand corner, was the return address. It read, "Mary Stoltzfus."

"Mary—this is from Mary?" Sarah's hands trembled as she gazed at the letter. Stunned and still not understanding how the letter had come to be in their mailbox, she tore open the envelope and drank in the words from her precious daughter. She read quickly as if she were afraid this was a dream and she'd awaken too soon. Then she sat back and read it again, trying to absorb every word.

It was too good to be true and, if Sarah had not known her daughter so well—the handwriting, the bubbly way the words spilled across the pages—she would have thought this was a cruel joke. But it was true! Mary was well, and she was happy. She'd even asked about her parents and—could it really be—that she and Jason were studying and discovering in God's word the same message as she and Eli?

Too shaken to back-up the car, she left it parked by the mailbox. Getting out, she walked slowly up the drive. She clutched the letter, still fearful that somehow it would vanish. She sat on the front steps of the house and read it again. And, as she read, the hard, grating, kernel of hurt, that had been her constant companion since Mary left, began to dissolve, and the tears fell uncontrollably as Sarah wept.

Eli's shirt clung to his back and sweat poured down his face, as the chainsaw cut into the last limb of the fallen oak. The saw whined to a stop, and Eli stacked the cut logs into the back of the pickup truck.

This wood will keep us warm through a good many winter days, he thought, as he turned the key in the truck's ignition. He swung the truck around slowly and headed for the woodshed. As he did, he looked down the long drive. The sight of Sarah's car parked at the edge of the road caught his attention.

His heartbeat quickened. "I thought Sarah had already left for town. I hope nothing is wrong."

Then he saw her sitting on the front steps. He swung open the truck door and hurried to her. She looked up with a tear-stained face and held the letter out to him and, in a voice tinged with disbelief, she said, "It's from Mary."

Eli held the letter in his hands, opened it slowly, and with a mixture of hope and dread began to read. His thoughts wrapped around each word, as its meaning impacted his mind. As he read, relief and thanksgiving filled his soul. A burden he'd carried inside since Mary left rolled away. God was giving him a chance to make things right with his daughter. He would beg for her forgiveness. Maybe they'd go to her, if she was open to their coming. He wasn't sure how—he'd received a warning from the CCC. Were there restrictions on their leaving the area? Would they be stopped if they tried to leave?

He needed time to think.

Sarah watched, curious as to what his reaction would be. He stood still, looking at the letter, and then he carefully folded it, handing it to her, and said, "I need to wash up; then we'll talk.

He stepped into the shower, turned the faucet, and waited for the pleasurable jolt of the icy water. Sarah could never understand why, even sometimes in winter, he preferred a cold shower. It had begun when, as a child, he'd come to the house after a long, hot, summer day of work and play. Dat would take a bucket of the cold well-water and slosh it over Eli and his brother so they could wash away the first layer of the day's grime before they entered the house. He'd discovered then that the anticipation of the shock the cold water would bring was the worst thing and that afterward one could enjoy an invigorating bath. So, he'd trained himself to look forward to the first burst of coldness.

If only it was that easy with the rest of one's life.

The cold jets of water stung his body, refreshing his tired muscles and clearing his mind.

He could see that God was working in this. He'd been more concerned about the warning than he'd let Sarah know. He was a peaceful man, and he was willing to suffer for his beliefs, but he didn't see any benefit in sitting and waiting for trouble—trouble he was sure was knocking at their door. He was most concerned for Sarah; would they arrest her, too? He'd already thought about their leaving for a while, but he didn't know where they should go. Now, he felt the letter from Mary was an answer. They'd certainly be thrilled to see Mary and, at the same time, they would escape, if only temporarily, the clutches of the local CCC.

Sarah cradled the phone in her hand. She needed to talk to Rachel, to find out about the letter. She must have put it in their mailbox, but why hadn't she called or left a note. Did she think they would be angry because she'd been in contact with Mary?

The phone rang several times before someone answered. "Hello," Rachel's voice greeted her.

"Rachel, honey, this is your mother, we need to talk." In the background, Sarah could hear Julie, but there was silence from Rachel and then a disconnection.

Sarah called again, but there was no answer. Guilt filled Sarah. She wondered, *How could she be happy about Mary, when Rachel and Tom were so angry with them?*

Eli came into the room and saw her standing there, staring at the phone. Putting his arms around her, he said, "We must remember that God loves our children even more than we do. We must trust. But now we need to talk about Mary."

They sat together, discussing the possibilities. First, they needed to call Mary. They had her address, and they hoped that her phone number would be listed; if not, they would do a search using the Internet. Eli shared with Sarah how he felt that God was opening a way for them—not only to see their daughter but to get away for a while. "I would like to see Mary," Sarah answered. "I'm sure, from her letter, that she isn't angry with us and will want us to come, but I don't want to escape just for myself—not if my staying will help someone. Do you think God would rather we stayed here and take a stand for what is right?"

"I've thought of that," Eli replied. "We've taken our stand, and I don't see why waiting to be fined and maybe arrested is going to help anyone. Of course, it's a long way to Colorado. When the CCC discovers that we've left, they'll probably have the use of our smart card canceled."

"We'd have to be careful about using it anyway," Sarah said. "That is if we don't want them to know where we are."

After a few more moments of discussion, Sarah opened the Internet search app on her phone, said a silent prayer for God's help, and keyed in Mary's name and address. Miraculously, it seemed to Sarah, a phone number popped up.

Eli put his hand on Sarah's. "Before we call, let's ask for God to give us His wisdom."

"Yes," Sarah agreed.

They knelt together, as they had done many times lately, and they poured out their hearts to God. They thanked Him for leading them and asked for His guidance and protection for them and their children.

They arose, feeling assured and decided to plan their trip before calling Mary. That way she would know when to expect them.

They decided they would leave Saturday after having worship with Amanda and Jonathan. They'd be the only ones who would know about their leaving. Eli would leave detailed instructions for Tom and would specify his desire to have the market closed on Saturday, the Sabbath. Eli could only pray that Tom would obey his father's wishes. Sarah would write to Rachel and tell her that they had decided to take a few days off. She'd plead with her to open her heart to God's calling and ask to see her when they got back.

Eli studied the atlas. If they left Saturday afternoon they could first drive to his cousin's home in Ohio. They'd spend Sunday with them and then leave Monday morning and try to stay Monday night at a great-aunt of Sarah's who lived in Illinois—just a few miles from St. Louis, Missouri. From there, they'd travel the more than 800 miles to Boulder, without stopping overnight again. This would get them to Mary's apartment by late Tuesday evening or early Wednesday morning. Since both of their relatives lived on farms, they hoped to obtain gasoline from them. Other times, they'd have to depend on the providence of God, since their smart card—they were sure—would be useless.

Mary Stoltzfus arrived home earlier than usual from her job at the gift shop. She loved working there. The enchanting dried flower arrangements, the scented candles, the pieces of driftwood—and other delightful things of nature which were fashioned into objects of beauty—they all filled Mary's senses. As she had at the family market, she shone when meeting the customers. Because it had a reputation of being a quality gift shop, they had many local patrons, but also quite a few tourists. Occasionally a family would come in, and Mary's heart would quicken when she saw the conservative dress and demeanor and recognized them as one of the plain people. The first time this happened, she was plagued with guilt and wondered what she would do if someone from her home came in, but, so far, the Mennonite or Amish shoppers who came into the store were all from the mid-West. She observed them as they looked at the beautiful, high-priced, but useless objects in the store and wondered what they were thinking.

Mary glanced around her apartment. It was Wednesday, and tonight they'd have the Bible study here. She smiled; it really wasn't their apartment anymore. Since Jason and she had begun studying the Bible, they'd made so many changes in their lives. One of those changes was for Jason to live somewhere else until they could be married. Bryan, a neighbor who had befriended them, lived in a nearby apartment; he also was attending the Bible studies and suggested that Jason move in with him for a while.

Mary's heart skipped a beat. In just a week and a half, they'd be baptized and then married at the end of the Sabbath. A perfect way to start a new life in Jesus. The jangle of the phone startled Mary from her thoughts.

"Hello."

"Is this Mary Stoltzfus?" Sarah asked with a trembling voice.

"Yes," Mary tensed. Her mind raced, trying to identify the familiar-sounding voice.

"Who's calling," she finally asked.

"Mary, this your mother and father."

"Mama," Mary whispered, afraid that if she acknowledged the familiar voice, it would vanish.

Her heart pounded and her mouth was dry. Had something awful happened? To Rachael, Jonathan, or Tom? Maybe it was Julie? –Rachel had said she was sick.

"Mary, there was an awkwardness in Eli's voice. "Please don't hang up on us. Your mother and I want you to know that we love you, and I am asking you to forgive me for dealing so harshly with you."

The guilt that plagued Mary for forsaking the traditions of her parents' religion had slowly dissolved, as she discovered the wondrous gift of God's grace. Yet, Mary knew that she had hurt her parents deeply. Now, she listened incredulously to her father's pleas for forgiveness.

"Papa, it is you who needs to forgive me. I acted rashly, and I know I hurt Mama and you. I've missed you both so much."

"We've all missed you," Sarah's voice broke in. "Rachel gave us your letter, and we want to come to see you—to be there for your baptism and wedding on Sabbath."

Mary hesitated, "You know the Sabbath is Saturday, the seventh day, not Sunday."

"We know," Sarah said.

THE WEBSTER FAMILY

Chapter Ten

Midnight in Mississippi

From Memphis, Tennessee, to St. Louis, Missouri, that Monday evening, September 6, was a typical late summer evening. In Memphis, the air hung warm and humid over Graceland, and partygoers on the riverfront lamented how it seemed there would never be a break from the summer heat.

In St. Louis, the Gateway Arch, illuminated against the black night sky, beckoned visitors to the city. Up and down the Mississippi River, barges plowed the waters, carrying goods from the Midwest south to the port of New Orleans and then traveling north again loaded with other cargo. Along the winding stretches of the river, watercraft from large yachts to small fishing boats rocked gently at their moorings, awaiting the morning.

The night grew late and, in hundreds of factories, hospitals, police and fire stations, shifts changed and weary workers headed home after being replaced by the night crews. The stream of traffic over the river's bridges gradually slowed, as the night grew late and thousands of lights in large cities, small hamlets, and rural homes went out as people turned off their computers and TVs and went to bed.

On that Monday evening in Byhalia, Mississippi, Kathy Webster paused from grading fourth-grade math papers and kissed her son Kevin goodnight.

Kevin shuffled toward the doorway and then stopped. "Mom?" "Yes, sweetie," Kathy answered, without looking up.

"Do you think Dad will come to my birthday party?"

Kathy put the papers on the coffee table and looked at her son. She could hardly understand how he had gotten so big—it seemed like just a moment ago that she and Cal were taking him home from the hospital, a small bundle who absorbed every moment of their time—at least Kathy's time. Even then, Cal had not been around very much when they needed him.

"Come here Kevin," she said, patting the seat next to her.

Kevin plopped down, and Kathy put her arms around him. "We've invited him, but you know your dad. He gets busy sometimes and...."

"But, Mom, he promised me this time. He said that being ten was an important birthday and that he'd be sure to come," Kevin exclaimed.

"Don't worry about it then, I'm sure he will," Kathy assured Kevin, while making a mental note to call Cal the next day and remind him of his promise.

Kathy rose and walked with Kevin to his bedroom, noticing his camping backpack laying by his bed. "Why is this here?" she asked puzzled.

"Oh, it's nothing—I just thought when Dad comes to my party I'd talk to him about us going camping sometime," Kevin mumbled.

"Kathy sighed and sat on the edge of Kevin's bed, "You miss the camping trips with your Dad, don't you?"

"I guess," Kevin shrugged.

Kathy remembered that camping was the one thing that had interested Cal and, after Kevin was older, they'd gone on several trips with him. Kevin had been a real little trooper, trying hard not to be a bother so that his dad would take them again sometime soon. She smiled, as she remembered the time they'd backpacked in the Smokey Mountains. They'd set up camp, and Cal was busy starting a campfire, when four-year-old Kevin very calmly said, "Dad, there's a bear."

Cal, knowing Kevin had talked about seeing bears all day, nodded without looking up and went on building the fire.

"Daddy, the bear's getting closer," Kevin stammered, his voice a little higher pitched this time.

Kathy had stuck her head out of their tent just in time to see Cal's reaction when he turned and saw a rather large bear walking nonchalantly toward them! Cal's startled shout, accompanied with much arm-waving and Kevin's, by then, excited screaming had almost given the poor beast a heart attack, and he went plunging past them, running up the hill into the woods. The last thing they saw of the bear was his rump bounding over the hilltop. They'd seen no other bears that trip, and they laughed together, while deciding that the bear had told all his friends to stay away from those crazy people! Kathy smiled. Yes, camping with Kevin and Cal was one of her good memories, also.

"I miss the backpacking trips, too; maybe now that I've finished school and have a teaching job, we'll have more time to do fun things," Kathy said, trying to be optimistic. "Maybe we can go visit Uncle Bryan. He's always wanting us to come and see him, and there are some awesome camping places in Colorado where he lives."

"Does Dad like Uncle Bryan?" Kevin asked.

Kathy hesitated, knowing Bryan hadn't cared for the way Cal had treated his big sister, "Of course he does."

"But Dad wouldn't go with us, would he?"

"Probably not," Kathy sighed, as she tucked the covers around Kevin.

Walking wearily back to the living room, she picked up the stack of papers and absentmindedly thumbed through them. After Cal left, maybe she should have moved to Colorado and been near her brother. Kathy and Bryan's parents had been killed in an automobile accident while Bryan was a senior in high school and Kathy had been in her third year of college. After the tragedy, Bryan had been her only focus. By the time she'd paid for the funeral and the debts her parents had left, very little insurance money remained. To make what was left go further, she'd quit college and gotten a full-time job. At times, it was tough and, without her parents or other close relatives to lean on, Kathy had drawn from an inner strength that, until then, she did not know she possessed. She was determined for Bryan to finish high school and college. Her time would come later, she reasoned, but then she'd met Cal. She remembered how her heart pounded the first time they'd met. His blond hair, deep blue eyes and boyish good looks, combined with a charismatic personality, had swept her off her feet. She should have realized that his charm was backed by total irresponsibility, but, after the numbness that had prevailed since her parents' death, it had felt so good to feel something inside again. She had put aside her misgivings and convinced herself that there was nothing to fear. Kathy sighed and put the math papers down. She'd held on for six long years, hoping Cal would grow up, but it was a vain hope. Her jaw clenched against the pain of remembering the day, three years ago, when her hopes had died. She'd suspected that there were other girlfriends—an accusation that Cal always denied—but, this time, he just looked at her and said bluntly, "It's not anything to do with you. I just don't want to be married anymore."

Then, without a backward glance, he'd picked up his car keys, took his jacket, and left. The next few weeks were a blur. She was given custody of Kevin and decided to stay in Byhalia; Cal moved to Memphis, Tennessee, but promised he would still be a part of his son's life. *Well, so much for promises*, Kathy thought. Maybe she should have listened to Bryan and moved to Colorado to be with her remaining family, but she'd felt Kevin needed to be closer to his dad. She knew the distance to Colorado would have been all the excuse Cal needed not to see his son. Not that he needed an excuse—his visits now were few and very far between. Kathy put the papers away and stretched. The muscles in her neck felt as if they were wound into a knot, and her head throbbed. She rose slowly and walked down the hall to her bedroom. Before getting ready for bed, she hung the slacks and shirt she would wear to school the next day over the chair by her bed. As she turned off the bedside lamp, a recent photo that she'd had taken of her and Kevin caught her eye. They stood together, mother and son—she, tall and slender, with dark eyes and hair, and Kevin with his father's blond hair and boyish grin. Kathy picked up the photo, "Kevin, I promise I will do everything I possibly can to get your father to come to your birthday party, but, if something should happen and he doesn't come, you shall have a terrific birthday anyway." The softness of the bed engulfed her, and Kathy slept.

> *Kathy didn't know which awakened her ... Kevin's screaming, the house shaking, or glass shattering*

Two hundred miles to the north, near New Madrid, Missouri, at exactly 2:00 a.m. on a Tuesday morning, the earth beneath the mighty Mississippi shifted with a violent thrust. As the ground above began to heave back and forth, a noise like terrible thunder rumbled through the land. From St. Louis to Memphis, brick buildings, mighty skyscrapers, and huge sports complexes collapsed. Automobiles plunged into the dark, murky river, as bridges buckled and massive gas lines ruptured, causing colossal explosions. In Arkansas, as the earth reeled, the swollen river was sucked backward and then pushed forward, erupting in a fifty-foot wall of water that swept away levees, causing floodwater to surge across hundreds of acres. As the shock waves spread outward, people as far away as Virginia to the east and Kansas to the west felt the impact.

Kathy didn't know which awakened her ... Kevin's screaming, the house shaking, or glass shattering. Alarmed, she flipped the switch on the bedside lamp; it flickered and then went out, leaving the room darker than before.

"Kevin, I'm right here. Are you alright?" she called, while frantically feeling for the sneakers she'd left under her bed.

"I think so," but something is on my legs," He said, his voice shaking.

"Listen to me Kevin, calm down and don't move until I get there."

She groped her way through the dark room. A sharp object scraped her arm, as she squeezed through the doorway. Kevin's room was across the hall. She heard him whimper. "I'm almost there. Remember, stay still."

"Mom, what happened? Did a tornado hit our house?"

"I don't know, but I think I know what's on your legs. It's the bookcase," Kathy replied.

As she felt her way around the bookcase, her leg bumped against something soft, but bulky. "I've found your backpack. Did you put your flashlight in it?"

"It's in the pocket on the right side," Kevin said.

"Bless you," Kathy replied, as she felt inside the pocket and grabbed the flashlight.

The flashlight beam revealed a room filled with debris. Anything attached to the wall had been jarred loose. Large and small objects had toppled, and broken glass was everywhere. Relief swept through her, as the light found Kevin. The bookcase had fallen across the foot of his bed, and books were strewn all around, but Kevin seemed unscathed.

Trying to hide the panic that she felt, she laughed, "You look a little silly lying there with all those books around you. Can you wiggle your toes?"

"Yes, ma'am. I can move my legs a little."

"Good. You hold the light and when I lift the case, you move your legs out of the way," she said, squeezing his hand for courage. "Here goes."

She put her shoulder to it and pushed against the bookcase. The case moved and things crashed around them. Kathy pushed harder, and Kevin jerked his legs free. They searched for his shoes. "You must wear these, or you'll cut your feet," Kathy said trying to clear her mind and think what else to take before leaving the house. Kevin slipped on his shoes and a pair of shorts and they quickly made it to the hallway.

"Mom, your arm is bleeding," Kevin exclaimed in alarm.

Kathy looked down at an ugly gash on her arm. She'd only felt a sting. "It'll be okay. I'll get a towel from my bathroom. Stay here and don't move," she instructed Kevin. The bathroom was a jumble of broken glass and bottles. Kathy grabbed a clean towel from the rack as she looked down at her arm. The bleeding seemed to have stopped, so maybe the cut wasn't as bad as it had looked to begin with. The nightshirt she was wearing was caked with blood. She looked around, realizing that she needed something else to wear, when she spied the shorts and shirt she had taken off earlier. She tore off the bloody shirt, being careful not to reopen the wound on her arm, and then quickly slipped on the shorts and shirt.

Suddenly, she jumped and Kevin screamed, as something outside exploded. She grabbed Kevin's hand, and they stumbled out the front door just as a low rumble sounded deep within the earth and the ground began to shake again.

"Quick, get out in the open," Henry Wade, a neighbor, shouted. Kathy and Kevin ran toward the street. Other neighbors were gathering there. The Wade's baby cried, and Margaret Wade jostled the infant, trying to comfort her. A small child sobbed. Kathy held Kevin tightly, while looking around.

Streetlights were out, and the only light on their block came from a few flashlights. A house in the next block was engulfed in flames, while, down the street, a tree had toppled onto electric lines and sparks were shooting out in all directions.

Men with flashlights began checking the houses on the block to make sure that no one was trapped. Kathy offered Kevin's flashlight to a helper. "I'll bring it back," the neighbor promised.

An unanswered question was on everyone's minds: *what's happened?*

"Couldn't have been a tornado," someone stated. "Maybe it was a terrorist attack on Memphis," another suggested, as they watched a red a glow in the northwest sky.

"The Robbins are from California, and they say it was an earthquake," Henry Wade reported.

"Earthquake?" The word hung in the air, formed out of disbelief. Then someone said, "It's the New Madrid quake—they've been predicting it for a number of years."

"You really think so?" Mrs. Wade asked, her voice lost as a rumble from somewhere deep in the earth grew louder and louder. The ground shook for what seemed like a lifetime until, at last, the shaking quit. Then there was a deadly silence, punctuated only by the distant wail of sirens.

Chapter Eleven

A Gray Morning

They stood stunned. They were accustomed to tornados. On many occasions, the wail of the warning siren would waken them to the report of a funnel cloud spotted in their county. Anyone who had lived in the area for any length of time had at least one tornado story to share—something they had seen or involving someone they knew. There were incredible tales of pine needles being driven through telephone poles; of a family's photo album, undamaged, being found in the next county; of someone's cow caught high in a tree, leaving the owner puzzled as to how to rescue the poor critter; and always, there were tales of narrow escapes from a twister's fury. Kathy remembered a school friend whose mobile home had been ripped apart while the friend and her mother hunkered, unscathed, in the bathtub with a mattress over them.

Tornados could be dealt with. They came and then it was over. But this was different.

There was nothing to see or hear—no black clouds or siren's wail. How could you know where it was coming from? How could you escape? Kathy remembered, from history lessons, that one of the worst series of earthquakes in the United States had occurred along the New Madrid Seismic Zone back in the early 1800s. The earthquakes had happened over a period of two years, but, because it was a time when very few people lived in the area, it was difficult to measure the damage. More recently, there had been a media stir when a man named Iben Browning, who had some scientific knowledge, had announced that another quake was due on December 3, 1990. For a while, the prediction generated interest in earthquake disaster preparedness. Then, December 3 passed without a tremor, and the quake became the greatest non-event of 1990. People went about their lives as usual—the only difference being that they now were aware of the possibility of a quake in the area.

The neighbor brought Kevin's flashlight back. Fire engulfed another home at the end of their block, and the flames cast angry shadows on the people gathered in the street. Volunteers ran to try to save some of the owner's belongings.

"Is our house going to burn?" Kevin asked.

"I don't think so," Kathy answered. "The electricity is off, and we don't have gas heat or appliances, so there is no gas line."

"What are we going to do?" Kevin asked, as his lip trembled; Kathy sensed his fear.

"First, we need to find a place to rest until morning, and then I'll see what I can rescue from the house and what condition it's in."

"How about our van?" Kevin suggested.

"Good idea." Kathy beamed the flashlight toward the van parked in their drive.

"I'm glad we have insurance," she murmured when she saw a large pine tree toppled across the back of the van.

"We can get in the front. The bucket seats will be a good place to rest."

"Will the ground shake again?" Kevin asked.

"Maybe. If Mr. Wade is right about this being an earthquake, then we'll probably having aftershocks, but they will not be as bad as the first shock," Kathy assured Kevin. "Now let's pretend we are going on a trip. You always like to sleep when we are traveling."

After a few more questions, Kevin became quiet, and she could hear his deep breathing. Exhausted, Kathy slept fitfully. She awoke with a start, as the van shook. This time, the tremor didn't last long, and she saw, in the gray morning light, that Kevin was still asleep.

The night seemed like a very bad dream, but the reality that the morning brought was much worse. She had to figure out what to do. She was the strong one. She'd been strong for Bryan and kept her hurt inside when their parents died. She'd done the same for Kevin when Cal left.

Her mind raced. She needed her cell phone. Bryan would hear about this and worry. She needed to call Cal, also. She wished she had grabbed her wallet and car keys last night. She wanted to hear for herself what had really happened. The car probably had too much damage to drive, but she could at least turn on the ignition so they'd have a radio.

The house wouldn't be safe to stay in if there continued to be aftershocks. What would they need to survive? *Think Kathy, think*, she kept telling herself, as she pressed her hands against her head. Food, water, and shelter—isn't that what she'd learned in Girl Scouts. She'd go back into the house. She'd been awakened by a tremor, but maybe there wouldn't be another one for a while.

She eased the van door open, stopping when Kevin moved.

"Mom, what happened?" Kevin asked, confused.

"We're still not sure. I'm going back into the house to get the things we need. You stay here. Do not follow me. Do you understand?"

"Please don't go!" Kevin wailed.

"I have to," Kathy answered, and then she paused. "Kevin, if something happens during all this—I mean if we get separated or something. You are to call Uncle Bryan; you know his number. He will know what to do."

"But Mom...," Kevin protested.

"I know everything will be okay, but just in case," she said, as she patted his hand. "Now remember, you are not to follow me into the house. Promise?"

"Yes ma'am--I promise," Kevin answered reluctantly.

A blanket of clouds wrapped the land in a wet mist, and smoke stung Kathy's nose as she opened the van door.

The house looked intact from the outside, but inside everything was in shambles. She picked her way through the broken glass, debris, and sagging ceiling, wondering how they had managed to get out with only a cut on her arm.

They needed water. She pushed away a fallen piece of cabinet and turned on the kitchen faucet—only a gurgle resulted. *The water mains must be broken*, she thought. There was some juice and a couple of bottles of water in the refrigerator. The refrigerator had already begun defrosting—but the juice, milk, and water were still cool. She saw the sandwiches she'd made for their lunch just the night before. So much had changed since then. She grabbed some apples and sliced cheese and placed them beside the juice, milk, and water. The peanut butter jar was still sitting on the cabinet, and she added that to her stash. She needed something to put the food in, and she thought of Kevin's backpack.

She made her way carefully down the hall to Kevin's room. It was hard to comprehend what had happened, as she looked at the tangled mess of her home.

His backpack lay on the floor at the foot of the bed. She looked it over and saw that Kevin had packed well. There was a tent, sleeping bag, mess kit, the Scout knife Cal had given him, a canteen, a hatchet, matches—even a small first-aid kit. *It was strange that Kevin had packed so many of the things they needed now,* Kathy thought.

Shouldering the backpack, she went quickly to her bedroom and gathered her cell phone, wallet, and a pillowcase. In the kitchen, as she stuffed food items into the backpack and pillowcase, as the house began to shake. A ceiling fan crashed to the floor beside her, as she dashed to the front door.

A wide-eyed Kevin greeted her outside.

"I thought I told you to stay in the van," Kathy barked.

"I wanted to help," Kevin stammered.

"Getting hurt isn't going to help,' Kathy snapped back. Her tone softened as she saw the hurt in Kevin's eyes. "I'm sorry," she said. "I just want you to be safe. Now, let's look and see what I got."

They spread their goods on the front lawn. "The phone is dead, but I can charge it in the car." She handed the bottle of orange juice to Kevin. "Sorry, no glasses," she said.

"There's a cup in my pack," Kevin replied.

She looked at Kevin. His hair was tousled, and there was a smudge on his face, but what she noticed was the sure way he unfastened the pack and took out the needed items. In his movements, she caught a glimpse of the man her son would become.

"Kevin, I was wondering what caused you to pack all this gear. I know you wanted to talk to your Dad about a camping trip—but you could have done it without packing all this stuff. It seems as if you were preparing for this."

She'd been so angry at God when her parents were killed. Then she had decided that her anger was wasted because God didn't exist. If He existed, she reasoned, He wouldn't allow such bad things to happen to people

Kevin nodded, "I'd thought about talking to Dad about going camping, but then, just three days ago, I started thinking about all the things I'd need, and I felt like I just had to pack everything. I wasn't sure what you'd think—so I didn't tell you."

Kevin looked at his mother. "Mom, do you believe God cares about us?"

The question surprised Kathy. She'd been so angry at God when her parents were killed. Then she had decided that her anger was wasted because God didn't exist. If He existed, she reasoned, He wouldn't allow such bad things to happen to people. Yet, at times, it had seemed that there was a presence sustaining her, giving her strength, when she felt she could not go further. She shook her head, "I don't know, Kevin. Why do you ask?"

"Well, when I went to Vacation Bible School last summer with Dillon, the teacher said God cares about everything that happens to us. She said He doesn't want bad things to happen, but right now Satan makes bad things happen to people, and God allows it, so everyone can see that God's way is best." Kevin sighed, "I don't understand all of what she said, but I remember her telling us that God will be with us and protect us." Kevin paused, "I was thinking, maybe God was helping us when he made me think about packing the camping gear."

"Maybe so," Kathy said, giving Kevin a hug and trying to hide the tears that welled up in her eyes.

"Let's see if we can hear some news," Kathy said, as she jumped up and headed for the van. At first, only static filled the airways, but after slowly turning the dial several times, an announcer's voice came through. "A violent earthquake has hit. Memphis is devastated. Heavy damage reported as far north as St. Louis. Only sketchy reports have been received from outlying areas."

The announcer's voice broke, "Thousands are feared dead." He continued, "If you are in an area affected by the earthquake, please stay outside and wait. Help will come." The radio crackled, and the announcer's voice faded.

Kathy looked at the white face of her son.

"Is my Dad dead?"

"I don't know, Kevin," Kathy answered softly.

"Mom, are we going to die?"

An icy fear filled her. She was a survivor—but what if this time she failed? Failed Kevin?

What if there was something she could do to save them but didn't? Darkness filled her mind, and she knew she had never felt so alone.

Chapter Twelve

The Blue Book

They spent the rest of the day waiting. The rain stopped, but a gray cloud of smoke hung close to the ground. Kevin wanted to put up the tent, and Kathy agreed. It would keep him busy, and it might be better than sleeping in the van. At least there was a screened tent door and window, and they could put the flaps up for ventilation without worrying about mosquitos. She didn't know how long it would be before they could get more water or food, so she decided to ration the liquids they had. There was almost a gallon of milk, a half-gallon of orange juice, and two 16-ounce bottles of water. They'd drink the milk first because it would spoil, then the juice. For food, they had the two meat-and-cheese sandwiches she'd made the day earlier, three extra slices of cheese, four apples, two granola bars, and a jar of peanut butter. Her mind was fuzzy, and she couldn't think how best to ration the food—but she did know they'd have to drink the milk and eat the sandwiches first.

"Let's eat the sandwiches with milk for breakfast," Kevin suggested. "Then we'll have as much milk as we can drink for lunch with an apple and the extra cheese. We could give the milk we can't drink to the Wades and then, for supper, we'll have granola bars, peanut butter, and orange juice."

"Sounds good," Kathy agreed. "That will leave us an apple, peanut butter, and water for breakfast. After that, maybe it will be safer to go back into the house." She put her arms around Kevin. "You're a big help," she said., "I don't know what I'd do without you."

Her arm ached. She'd forgotten about the cut, but now the skin around it had turned red. She took the first-aid kit out of Kevin's pack and cleaned the cut. Kevin wanted to help her bandage it, and she let him. She had charged the phone, and she'd repeatedly tried to get through to Cal and Bryan, but there was only a rapid buzzing on the line. Later, a plea came over the radio for people to stop trying to use their cell phones. The overuse was clogging the channels and making it impossible for anyone to complete a call. "Please," the announcer pleaded, "Only use your phone if it is a life-or-death situation."

Henry Wade and several other men on the block began carrying guns with them. "Got to protect what is mine," Wade explained. "I heard looters already broke into a couple of houses two blocks over."

Kathy shivered—now there was something else to have to worry about.

Later that day, a plane swooped low over their neighborhood. White papers drifted down containing instructions. The National Guard Armory was being set up as a disaster-relief center. Everyone must report there the next morning. They were instructed not to try to drive. Not all of the bridges had been checked for safety; power lines were down, and many streets had buckled and were impassable. The paper said that it was important for all citizens to report—no matter their needs—so that the government could know the number of survivors. Each person was to bring the national I.D card. The rumors were that the Homeland Defense Department was concerned that terrorists would take advantage of the situation, and so everyone was being checked.

The day ended as dismally as it had begun. Rain fell again, harder than in the morning. She and Kevin debated on whether to sleep in the van or the tent. Kevin insisted on the tent, and Kathy gave in. She lay on the mat that Kevin had unrolled for her to use.

"I don't mind the ground," he said, and Kathy saw the look of satisfaction on his face when she accepted the mat.

He's trying to take care of me, Kathy thought. It seemed as if he was growing up before her very eyes. They lay on top of the unfolded sleeping bag and used a throw that was in the van to cover themselves.

She listened to the rain and thought of the hundreds of people still trapped in their homes. Was Cal one of them? What if Kevin's vacation Bible school teacher was right? Was there a God who cared about them? Would He listen to her if she asked Him to take care of Cal? Did Bryan know what had happened, and could it be that he was praying for Kevin and her? She didn't know how Bryan felt about God. They hadn't talked about it much after their parents' death. Their parents hadn't been the church-going kind. They had been raised in different faiths and had decided, when they got married, that it would be best not to attend any church. The only time Kathy could remember going to church was with their housekeeper and babysitter, Mrs. Mattie. She smiled. She was sure God had been a personal friend of Mrs. Mattie's.

Kathy's clothes clung to her in the dampness. She needed a bath. She and Kevin were both dirty—although Kevin didn't seem to mind. She silently took inventory of their situation.

They had enough to eat. They had shelter. Several times during the day, the ground trembled, and they'd waited in tense silence until the shaking stopped. She had no idea what tomorrow would bring—but, at this moment, they were safe. Perhaps that was all she could ask. She fell into an exhausted sleep.

The noise penetrated through the fogginess of Kathy's slumber—the sharp retort of a gunshot and the sound of men yelling.

Kevin stirred, "Mom, what's happening?"

"Shh...," Kathy whispered.

More shuffling, another gunshot, and then footsteps, pounding the ground, coming toward them. Kathy squeezed Kevin's hand. "Pray, Kevin," she whispered.

The footsteps came nearer. They stumbled; someone cursed. A dark shadow passed the tent, the footsteps faded, and then there was silence.

"You alright over there?" Melvin Wade's voice cut through the silence.

"We're okay," Kathy yelled back.

She did not sleep for the rest of the night.

The rain stopped sometime after that, and the sun rose, looking like a huge red ball through the smoky haze.

They ate breakfast quietly. Kathy felt an uneasiness. Would they be allowed to come back home? They rented the house, and so she had no idea what the owners would do about repairs. Kevin wanted to take the backpack—just in case they needed something. She saw it was important to him and agreed.

They all walked together—strangers, neighbors, friends, and families. She felt like one of the refugees she'd seen a picture of from some war-torn, third-world country. She remembered the despair she'd seen in their eyes as they carried their belongings in carts or on their backs, while mothers held tightly to their children. She'd never dreamed that she, nor her neighbors, would suffer such a fate.

They walked past homes that had been damaged in much the same way as theirs. In other areas, fire had destroyed whole blocks. After a while, they walked past a neighborhood that didn't seem to have suffered as much damage, and the owners had already started clearing away the debris. A pile of discarded items lay on the curb.

"Look, Mom," Kevin exclaimed.

Kathy looked as Kevin pulled a discarded hard-bound book from the rubble.

"It's a Bible story book. Can I keep it? Please. The people threw it away, but it's only a little wet on the edges."

Memories flooded Kathy's mind, as she flipped through the pages of the book Kevin handed her. She saw Mrs. Mattie's kind face. "Coming again, coming again, Jesus is coming again," she remembered the people at Mrs. Mattie's church singing those words. The reason she and Bryan had gone to church with Mrs. Mattie was that Mattie Johnson had explained to Kathy's parents that she went to church on Saturday, the Sabbath, and that she'd only keep the children on Saturday if she could take them to church with her. Kathy's parents had agreed. Going to church hadn't been as bad as Kathy and Bryan had anticipated. Even energetic Bryan had enjoyed the children's class. After church and the "fellowship" dinner they always had, Kathy remembered going home with Mrs. Mattie. They'd sit on the porch and Mrs. Mattie would bring out her special blue *The Bible Story* books and read them story after story. She remembered Bryan had liked the stories about Moses the best. She'd been fascinated with the stories of Jesus's return. When Kathy and Bryan had questions, Mrs. Mattie patiently answered them. The stories from those books had seemed so believable.

"May I keep the book? Please." Kevin interrupted her thoughts.

"Yes, you may keep it," Kathy answered thoughtfully as she handed the blue *The Bible Story* book back to him.

THE STOLTZFUS FAMILY

Chapter Thirteen

Apprehension

In Boulder, Colorado, Tuesday morning, September 7, dawned bright and clear. To the east, the early morning sun's rays cast long shadows on the rolling plains. During the night, the Rocky Mountains along the Front Range had received a dusting of snow at the higher elevations and their peaks glowed with iridescence as the rays of light touched them. Mary Stoltzfus turned in bed and looked at the clock—it was six o'clock already, and she had a ton of things to do before she went to work at the shop. A tinge of excitement crept up her spine. It was hard to believe her parents would be in her apartment this very evening. Eli and Sarah were early risers, and she knew they would leave the great aunt's home early so they could get through St. Louis before the morning rush hour.

At first, Jason had been wary of Mary's parents' unexpected visit, but Mary's excitement was contagious. Her eyes sparkled, and Jason thought she might start dancing around the room as she exclaimed, "They aren't angry, Jason. I can hardly believe Papa has studied and discovered the same things in God's Word that our group has been studying. It's incredible that they have come to believe as we do."

Jason put his arms around her, "I don't think I've ever seen you so happy. Then, with a stern expression before he broke into a grin, he said, "In fact, Mary Stoltzfus, I think I'm jealous."

Mary looked into his face, "Now I know you're teasing me. But I've even suspected that you, too, felt bad about the grief we caused everyone when we left."

Jason replied, "My parents were not happy, but they finally saw what a great person you were. In some ways, their acceptance of our behavior made me feel worse because I still had a connection with my family, while you were cut off from yours. I blamed myself for allowing you to be hurt."

"Well, you didn't force me to go with you. I made that decision, but that's in the past. When I ran away from my parents' home, I thought I'd left God, but, the wonderful thing is, He never left me or you. He was patiently waiting until the time was right for us to respond."

Jason agreed, "You're right. I can see how He has been leading us all along."

Mary jumped from the bed and headed for the bathroom. She'd already been in a whirl getting ready for the baptism and wedding, but now her parents' coming had added to the intensity. The phone's ring startled her. "Hello, this is Mary."

"This is Bryan. Have you turned on the television news this morning?"

"No, why?" Mary answered. Sometimes she didn't turn the television on right away. She resented its intrusion into her life, especially with the constant stream of bad news from around the world. *Maybe the Amish have the right idea—no television*, she'd thought to herself.

"There's been an earthquake."

"Where?" Mary asked cautiously, as she heard the tension in Bryan's voice.

"It happened along the New Madrid fault line. Have you ever heard of that?"

"I think so, but I don't know much about it."

"It's between St. Louis and Memphis. From the initial reports, it looks bad," Bryan replied.

"St. Louis?"

"Look, I'm worried," he continued, "I have a sister who lives 30 miles south of Memphis—just over the border into Mississippi—and I know your parents might be somewhere near St. Louis. Jason's already gone to work, but if it's okay with you I'm going to call the pastor. Maybe he can get some members together for special prayer, not only for our families but for all those who are affected."

Mary was silent. Fear froze her hand to the phone and left her speechless. Her mind raced. "Please God, be with my parents and Bryan's sister," she pleaded silently.

"Mary," Bryan's voice sounded as if he was miles away. "Yes," she whispered.

"I'm going to call the pastor and then I'm coming over—we'll watch this thing together if that's okay with you."

"Sure," Mary answered.

They watched the television intently. First reports were coming in from St. Louis, which had suffered severe damage, but not as extensively

Apprehension | 79

as towns further south. Nothing mattered to Mary except her parents' whereabouts. "Thousands feared dead, bridges out, roads buckled, explosions, aftershocks...." The words and pictures ran together in one continuous line of horror.

Throughout the country, businesses closed. The nation, already numbed by a series of natural disasters and terrorist attacks, watched in horror as the latest calamity unfolded.

Between news of the earthquake, scenes of protest and rioting in Europe flashed across the screen. Newscasters, as well as several prominent European scientists, were agreeing with the Russian astronomers about the danger of an asteroid hitting the earth. In the Middle East, the dreaded disease, which had afflicted so many in Europe and the United States, was raging. Mary and Bryan heard about a meeting that had been scheduled between the Muslim leaders and the Reverend Stone.

Jason came as soon as he heard the news. His boss did not protest but insisted Jason go and be with Mary. Part of Mary was happy that Jason was there, but seeing him also intensified the guilt she had begun feeling as soon as she realized her parents might be in danger. *God's punishing me for my disobedience to my parents*, she thought.

She arose and began pacing the floor. She wanted to run away from the awful darkness threatening to engulf her. Pictures of the peaceful life she'd left behind flashed through her mind. She remembered the good times they'd had working together. She saw the little church and her friends. She saw her parents' faces—she imagined the tears in Sarah's eyes when she'd ran away. She'd thrown it all away and nothing would ever be the same again. "It's all my fault, my fault," she anguished.

> *If what we're studying and have come to believe is Bible truth, then why is God punishing me and my parents? It's your fault for coming here and my fault for searching for something different*

Pastor Paul Stanley was an intense, tall, thin man whose life portrayed his desire to help lead his flock through the troubling times they were experiencing. Bev and Elizabeth, the students who were studying the Bible with Mary, Jason, and Bryan came with him to the apartment.

Pastor Stanley saw the grief on Mary's face as she approached him. She lashed out, "If what we're studying and have come to believe is Bible truth, then why is God punishing me and my parents? It's your fault for coming here and my fault for searching for something different," she cried.

The pastor withstood her tirade, and then he said gently, "Mary, fear is controlling your thoughts. God can take your fear and guilt, but you must let Him. God has forgiven you of your sins, and you must not let the evil one discourage you. Whatever happens, it is not your fault. Our lives are in God's hands and we must trust Him with them."

Mary looked into his kind, concerned face. She felt the struggle within, felt the suffocating, dark despair. "Can we pray?" she asked.

The group knelt and, as they prayed, a sense of peace filled their hearts. Mary's courage was renewed.

"Thank you," she whispered. "Please forgive me," she added, and the group embraced her with hugs.

Mary looked at her watch—it was noon and still no call from her parents. How could time go so slowly?

"I don't know if I should call someone from home or not—maybe Jonathan?" she questioned. "My parents indicated they might be in some trouble with the CCC for closing the market on Saturday. I remember them saying Jonathan would be the only one who knew they were leaving."

"If that's the case, it might be better to wait awhile," Pastor Stanley advised. "The CCC has a lot of power in other parts of the country. We haven't experienced that here because they have met resistance from some of our more free-spirited, independent minded-citizens."

As planned, Eli and Sarah left their home in Pennsylvania on Saturday afternoon, after giving Jonathan final instructions. On the way out of town, they mailed two letters—one to Rachel and another to Tom. Eli told Tom he was leaving him in charge of the store while he and Sarah took a few days off. He expressed his sorrow about the tension between them and pleaded with Tom to study his Bible and to ask God to lead him in all things.

Sarah read over the letter to Rachael one last time before she sealed it. "Please God touch her heart," she silently prayed.

Eli reached to hold Sarah's hand as they drove away. After a few moments of silence, he said, "I never thought we would have to keep secrets from our children about our whereabouts."

Sarah looked at him with a tear-stained face and squeezed his hand.

Matthew and Anna Stoltzfus were surprised, but cordial when Eli called Friday evening to say they were coming by for a visit. Eli and Matthew had grown up together until they were age ten, and then

Matthew's parents had purchased a farm in Ohio and moved away. The visit gave the men time to reminisce about their boyhood. On Sunday, Eli and Sarah attended church with Matthew and Anna. Afterward, Eli tried to talk with them about spiritual matters, but they seemed uninterested. Sarah noticed Anna only wore her plain clothes to church but dressed quite fashionably the rest of the time.

They left Eli's cousin's home early Monday morning.

A smile lighted Great-Aunt Sarah's weathered face when she greeted Sarah, her great-niece and namesake. The questions flowed as she invited them in—how were the children and grandchildren? The farm? She'd heard about the drought. Their problem in Illinois was too much rain. Sarah was amazed at the agility of the woman, who, although nearing ninety years old, still kept up a large vegetable garden and possessed a quick wit. Sarah sensed her great-aunt was happy to see them, but she thought she caught a flicker of surprise in her eyes when she looked out and saw Eli bringing in the luggage from their truck.

Eli sat in the living room while Sarah and her great-aunt prepared the evening meal. A large-print, Bible sat on a table. Eli noticed that the Bible was opened to Revelation, and beside it was a study guide entitled, *Amazing Facts,* which Eli began to read, his curiosity building.

Great-aunt Sarah invited Eli to say grace, and they bowed their heads together. Before they began eating, Great-Aunt Sarah cleared her throat and said nervously, "I must tell you something. I feared you would think I'm just a foolish old woman, and so I was going to keep silent, but I can't."

Eli interrupted, "We'd never think that, Great-Aunt...."

Great-Aunt Sarah looked at him, "Now don't be interrupting an old woman or she might get cold feet and not say what must be said. First, I've been studying my Bible a lot lately, and I am convinced that Jesus is going to come soon. I've felt His presence with me as I study, but I never thought he'd send me a message—that is until last night. I had a dream, and it was a message for the two of you."

"A message for us?" Sarah interrupted.

Great-Aunt Sarah held her hand up, "Let me finish. God told me that you must not stay here. I was to feed you and then send you away because you must travel past St. Louis before ten o'clock tonight. I wasn't going to tell you. I thought I was being foolish, and then I saw your truck and it was exactly like I had seen in the dream! I had no idea what you would be driving and, when I saw it, I knew the dream was real and that I must tell you."

After a moment, Eli said, "You did right, and we understand—we've been studying our Bible also, and we know God is leading us."

Then Eli, Sarah, and Great-Aunt Sarah begin to share the marvelous ways in which God was working in their lives. A few hours later, Sarah and Eli left Great-Aunt Sarah's home, spiritually and physically renewed. Their truck was filled with gas, and there was enough food to do them for a week.

At 9:30 p.m., they drove over the Mississippi and passed by the Gateway Arch. Sarah said, "I was hoping we'd have time to stop and look it over, but I guess God had other plans."

"I wonder why," Eli mused.

For Mary and the friends gathered in her apartment, time blurred. The news media brought continuing updates. People came and went. Someone brought food—but still, there was no phone call. Bryan had managed to stay calm, but now he began to pace the floor—the news from the Memphis area was not encouraging.

The phone's sharp ring startled them.

"Hello," Mary answered.

"Mary, this is your father."

"Papa?" Mary's heart quickened.

"God has protected us," Eli proclaimed. "We're at the Colorado state line, and we'll be at your apartment sometime tonight."

THE WEBSTER FAMILY

Chapter Fourteen

Homeless

The lines in front of the armory were long. Kathy saw a few of her students and their parents.

"There is my teacher," one child explained, as she tugged on her mother's arm. The mother looked and smiled at Kathy. The smile did not disperse the haggard look on her face.

"I must look a mess," Kathy thought, as she rubbed her fingers through her hair. She concluded, "A bath and clean clothes would be heaven-sent."

"Do you think they'll have food?" Kevin asked.

"Probably apples and peanut butter. I hear it's becoming a fad," Kathy teased.

"Oh Mom," Kevin moaned.

TV monitors had been installed inside the armory. Kathy was stunned at the destruction that flashed across the screen. She and the others who entered the armory fell silent as they saw, for the first time, the scope of the disaster.

The news coverage was interrupted by a message from the President. The President, several cabinet members, and the CCC leader appeared on the screen.

"Citizens of our great country," the President began in a sober tone. "Two days ago, our nation suffered the worst natural disaster in our history. We do not yet know the final death toll, nor the monetary loss. This disaster has the potential of bringing our nation to its knees. East/west ground transportation has been virtually brought to a halt. Major oil and natural gas pipelines have been severed. Dams and locks have been destroyed, which means that barge traffic on the Mississippi River has come to a halt. Millions of homes and businesses have been destroyed."

The President paused and continued, "But we are prepared. Several years ago, when the possibility of such a disaster was discussed, a New

Madrid Relief Plan was designed. That plan is now in place." The President went on to explain how the plan would work and emphasized that everything possible was being done to find and care for the victims. He ended his speech with a special appeal. "Let's remember that God is in control of all things. For years now, our fellow Americans in the Concerned Citizen's Council have warned this nation that, if we did not turn back to God, something of this magnitude would happen. One of the first steps to show our allegiance to our Creator is to observe His Sabbath, which is Sunday the Lord's Day. The local chapters of the CCC have worked tirelessly to ensure that our citizens worship on the Lord's Day, and they have censored those who obstruct in any way the observance of the Sabbath. With this in mind, I, with the help of our CCC leaders and the members of Congress, have signed into effect a new law. We are calling the bill the Unity Law because it is designed to unify us as one people under God. The first facet of this law declares this coming Sunday to be a special day of worship and prayer for our nation. I want each citizen to commit to observing this day. The United States of America was founded as a nation under God. We have strayed from this calling. Now, it is each citizen's responsibility to turn back to God, to recommit to worship Him, and to uphold the moral standards of His law. Those who do not will be dealt with as enemies of our country.

> *For years now, our fellow Americans in the Concerned Citizen's Council have warned this nation that, if we did not turn back to God, something of this magnitude would happen*

People had crowded into the armory when the President began to speak. Everyone stopped to listen. Kathy felt comforted by his words to start with but, for some reason—she couldn't quite put her finger on it—when he began talking about God and worshiping him on His day, she felt uncomfortable. Was it because she hadn't thought about her relationship with God? She'd never taken Kevin to church and, if she did, what church would it be? There was something else though, something she couldn't quite remember which made her feel uneasy. There was loud applause and many *amens* when the President finished.

Good morning, ma'am. May I see your ID card?" the man asked, as Kathy approached the first table. Kathy handed him hers and Kevin's cards. The cards were checked by the computer, and the man smiled and handed them back. "There are phones if you need to call family," the man said and pointed to a row of phones. "You are limited to five minutes and two calls. After your phone calls, please go to station two," the man said, pointing to the next area. "If you don't need to make any calls, you may go there now. I hope things work out well for you ma'am," he added.

"Thank you. If I can't get in touch with my son's father in Memphis, who should I call? We're worried."

"The Red Cross will help. Their number is posted by the phones."

"Are we going to talk to Daddy?" Kevin asked.

"We are going to try," Kathy replied. "You know if there is no answer it may mean he is in a shelter or something."

"How will we know?"

"We may not know for a while, but there are people who will help us," Kathy assured him.

Her heart pounded and her mouth was dry as she dialed the familiar number. There was no response. The lady at the Red Cross was sympathetic as she took Cal's name, address, and phone number. Kathy held the line while the woman checked to see if Cal's name was on any of her lists.

She came back on the line, "His name isn't on anything here. If you could check back tomorrow, we'll have an updated list of the hospital and other agencies."

The call to Bryan was more productive.

"Sis!" Bryan was ecstatic. "I've tried to reach you by phone, and I prayed you were alright. I was so worried."

Kathy's heart warmed at his concern. Her pent-up emotions spilled out as she described the dreadful night of the quake, how she and Kevin were able to get out of the house, and how they had managed until the present.

"I haven't found out anything about Cal," Kathy said. Bryan was concerned.

"Whatever happens with Cal, I want you and Kevin to come and stay with me. I know we don't have time to talk about it now, but unusual things are happening in the world. We never went to church much when we were kids, but my neighbors, Mary and Jason and I have been studying the Bible with a couple of girls who came to Mary's apartment. They were working their way through college by selling some magazine-like books about the Bible. Do you remember those blue *The Bible Story* books that Mrs. Mattie used to read to us?

"Yes," Kathy answered. "Why?"

"Well, some of the books they were selling looked just like that."

"That's interesting," Kathy replied, as she looked at Kevin clutching *The Bible Story* book he had found.

"Bryan, I have to hang up now. Others are waiting in line. I'll call you as soon as I find out what we can do."

"Okay, Sis."

"And Bryan, keep praying for us."

Kathy hung up the phone and walked to the next station.

"We're here to establish your immediate needs and to help you find safe lodging," the woman at the table explained. "We need to know how much damage your home has sustained and, if it isn't livable if you have any other plans. Here is a questionnaire. Complete it, and it will help us determine how to handle your case."

Kathy took the questionnaire. It seemed so impersonal. They would determine how to handle her case—as if this was her fault. The questionnaire was long, and a weariness sank into her bones as she looked at the lines that began to blur together. Kevin was restless.

"I'm hungry," he said.

The woman at the table heard him and replied with a smile, "We'll be serving meals within an hour."

Kathy finished filling out the questionnaire. As she went to hand it to the woman, she was redirected by her to a man who quickly skimmed over the form.

Without looking up, the man said, "I think, from the damage you've described, that the house is not safe for you to live in at the present. We are setting up tents for the homeless, but, because of crowded conditions, it would be better to stay with friends or relatives if you have someone who lives nearby."

"We'd like to go and live with my brother who is in Colorado. Is it possible to get a flight?" Kathy asked.

The man shook his head, "Not for several weeks. All airports are being used as emergency supply routes. Is there anyone else?" Kathy shook her head, and the now-familiar dark, cold, aloneness filled her soul.

Chapter Fifteen

Mrs. Mattie Johnson

Robert and Carol Drake's home had not suffered any major damage during the quake, so they responded immediately when asked to help with the disaster relief. Their assignment was the armory in Byhalia, Mississippi, which was about 40 miles north of their home.

More than twenty-five years earlier, Robert Drake had put away his carpenter tools and picked up a briefcase. During those years, he had crisscrossed the roads of rural, northern Mississippi with one purpose in mind—to share the last-day message of the Bible with everyone he met—the message that was made clear through the religious books he carried in his briefcase. When Robert retired, he lay down his briefcase, but not his desire to love and help others. When Carol asked if he would like to attend Disaster Relief Response training classes sponsored by their church, and he readily agreed to go with her.

The Drake's expertise, when it came to disaster relief, was to set up and manage warehouses where donated goods could be distributed to victims in an orderly fashion. This area of relief help was a behind-the-scenes effort and did not often get the media attention that other areas of aid received. The Drakes and the other volunteers who helped them did not mind—it was not their purpose to receive attention. Because the earthquake had affected many and the need was so tremendous, the Drakes were asked to come immediately to the armory. Carol was showing a new volunteer around when she saw Kevin, standing alone, looking curiously at the throngs of people around him. He did not appear to be lost, and she would have passed him by had she not spotted the blue *The Bible Story* book that Kevin clutched tightly in his arms.

Asking the new trainee to wait a moment, Carol knelt beside Kevin, "Hi, young man, what is that you have?"

Kevin explained how he had found the book. "Is this your book?" he asked. "I didn't mean to take it if someone wanted it. I like it because of the pictures of Jesus. Let me show you. Mom said this one was a picture of Jesus coming back to earth," Kevin explained, as his clear, blue eyes looked intently into the face of Carol Drake. "I think it would be nice if Jesus came right now. Don't you? He could help me find my dad."

"Yes, I certainly do," Carol said, as she took the book Kevin handed to her and quickly explained some of the pictures. "I'm glad you found this book. I believe Jesus wants you to have it," she said, as she handed it back to him. "Before my husband retired, he sold books like this to a lot of families with boys just like you."

Kathy was engaged in a discussion with the man at the assignment table. "Can we at least go get some of our belongings?" she pleaded.

The man paused and Kathy looked around, suddenly aware that Kevin wasn't by her side. Panic filled her, as her eyes frantically scanned the crowd. The panic was replaced by relief when she spied Kevin showing someone his book.

Kathy sighed. She was puzzled about the significance of that book to Kevin. The only time he'd had to look at the book was while they waited in line. Since there wasn't time to read the stories, he'd asked questions about the pictures. She'd tried to explain as much as she could remember, but it had been a long time since she had sat at Mrs. Mattie's feet listening to her read those same stories.

"Kevin," Kathy admonished.

"I hope I haven't caused any trouble," Carol apologized, as she stood to greet Kathy.

Carol's friendly, gray eyes greeted Kathy's dark anxious ones. Kathy observed the motherly looking woman with laugh lines at the corners of her mouth and eyes.

I suspect this lady can see the humor in just about everything, Kathy supposed, and she felt comforted by the thought of it.

"I'm Carol Drake and my husband Robert and I are volunteer helpers here," Carol explained, looking down at the bright yellow shirt she wore with the Adventist Disaster Response logo stamped on the front.

Kathy stared at the shirt. She remembered sitting in the recreation room of Mrs. Mattie's little church. "We need to be ready to help those who need it," Mrs. Mattie had explained, and Kathy recalled how pleased Mrs. Mattie had been when Kathy had offered to help put the little bottles of shampoo, bars of soap, deodorant, toothpaste, and toothbrushes into plastic bags with drawstrings. Mrs. Mattie's wrinkled brown face had glowed, as her calloused hands handed Kathy several bags to fill. Kathy recalled that the bags had had the same logo on them as Carol Drake's shirt—Adventist Disaster Response.

"I'm sorry, is something wrong?" Carol asked, puzzled at the expression on Kathy's face.

"No, I was just remembering something. Do you know Mrs. Mattie Johnson?"

Carol was surprised at the question but tried to conceal it. "I sure do. Many years ago, Robert, my husband, sold her a set of Bible books, like the one Kevin has. We studied the Bible with her, and she became a Christian. She even helped start a church in her community."

"I've been to Mrs. Mattie's church," Kathy said softly.

Carol was more than surprised because the church was a small one with only about fifty members—most of them elderly now. Carol looked at Kathy. She was young, educated, and probably affluent. Her dark hair framed her pale skin. The likelihood that Kathy had attended Mrs. Mattie's church seemed—well, almost impossible.

"You have?" Carol exclaimed. "Let me get Robert; he'll want to hear how you know Mrs. Mattie," she continued, as she glanced in the direction of the new trainee and saw that another volunteer had taken over.

Robert and Carol invited Kathy to come with them to a cubicle that had been set up for the volunteers. Carol offered Kevin some milk and cookies. Kevin accepted without hesitation.

Kathy was overwhelmed by the way the Drakes seemed to care for each other and the loving and kind way they were treating her. For the second time that day, she poured her heart out. She told how she and Kevin had escaped from the house. She told about the backpack Kevin had felt impressed to pack beforehand. She explained how she knew Mrs. Mattie. She told them of her parents' untimely death. How she'd survived for Bryan's sake and how angry she'd been at God. She told them of Cal, their divorce, and how she worried about Kevin. The Drakes listened patiently and sympathetically.

When Kathy finally finished, Carol asked, "How would you and Kevin like to stay with Mrs. Mattie until you can go to your brother's house?"

A picture of Mrs. Mattie's sprawling, unpainted farmhouse with the large pecan trees surrounding it popped into Kathy's mind.

"Is she still—I mean she wasn't young when…."

"She still isn't young," Carol laughed. "But she is still quite alive. She may have a few more aches and pains than when she took care of you, but she is still taking care of her garden and any stray animal or person who crosses her path. I think she has already opened her doors to at least one homeless family, and I am sure she will be delighted to have you and Kevin stay with her. What do you think?"

"It would be so good to see her again! What do you think, Kevin?" Kathy asked.

"How will Dad know how to find us?"

"We'll let the Red Cross people know where we are staying," Kathy assured him.

"How will I find out about Cal?" Kathy asked. "Does Mrs. Mattie still have telephone service?"

"Probably not," Robert answered. "But I'll check every day and let you know when we find out anything."

"How can we get to Mrs. Mattie's? and...," Kathy hesitated.

"Yes?" Carol said.

"Can we go back to our house to retrieve a few things."

"First, we need to let the authorities know where you are staying," Robert stated. "I can get clearance to take you to Mrs. Mattie's home and to go by your house. Of course, no one can go inside unless, after inspecting it, I give the okay."

"At one time, Robert built houses," Carol injected. "So he'll know how sound a structure is."

"Let's get you some food while Robert gets the paperwork done," Carol suggested.

"One other thing," Kathy added. "I'll need to call Bryan to let him know where we are staying.

"I'll make arrangements for a call," Robert agreed.

They ate with relish the spaghetti, salad, and garlic bread provided—and ice cream bars for dessert! Kathy was thankful for the hard-working volunteers who served them.

After a while, Robert came back with papers for Kathy to sign, stating where she was staying and what her future intent was. Robert also had clearance for them to go back to see their house.

Bryan was excited when he heard where Kathy and Kevin would be staying.

"I can't think of any place I'd rather you'd be staying, other than with me," he said. "Kathy, open your heart to the things that Mrs. Mattie teaches you. She knows more concerning the things that are happening around us than I do."

"I don't understand," Kathy answered, puzzled.

"You will, Kathy. I know that all of this is more than coincidence. God has led you to Mrs. Mattie's."

"I can see that, too," Kathy replied.

"I'm praying for you and Kevin and Sis…if you don't get to come—if things close down before you can, I'll see you in the Kingdom."

"Bryan, what are you talking about?"

"Mrs. Mattie will explain! Bye, Sis. I love you." Kathy was shaken by the call. What did Bryan mean? Did he think he wouldn't see them again? In the Kingdom—what did that mean? Well, she'd certainly have plenty of questions for Mattie Johnson.

Her house was the way Kathy remembered it. Mrs. Mattie answered the door, and the Drakes introduced Kathy and Kevin to her. "My little Kathy! Child, how you've grown. Just look at you and such a fine son." Tears filled Mrs. Mattie's eyes, as she embraced Kathy and Kevin. "I've wondered about my Kathy and Bryan. Didn't know whatever happened to you. Heard you and your parents moved away to Memphis."

They talked non-stop for a few moments, and then Mrs. Mattie said, "Come on in and let me get you settled. Looks like a hot bath and some rest in a real bed would make both of you feel better. There'll be plenty of time to talk afterward."

"One thing," Kathy hesitated.

"Yes."

"Bryan said you'd be able to explain the things that are happening in the world today. He said he might not see me until we were in the Kingdom, but for me to open my heart to what you had to say. Do you know what he was talking about?"

"And can we read the stories in my book about Jesus," Kevin asked, holding up *The Bible Story* book for Mrs. Mattie to see.

"We'll have plenty of time for that. The Lord is good to bring you here so I can teach you these things," Mrs. Mattie said, as tears streamed down her face.

The hot bath was wonderful. Kathy lay between the clean sheets of the bed. Outside the world was falling apart, but here there was peace.

THE STOLTFUS FAMILY

Chapter Sixteen

Mary

Mary placed the note on the kitchen table where her parents would be sure to see it. She'd carefully written the instructions, so that they could find everything they needed for breakfast and had sketched a map, showing how to get to the shop where she worked.

Eli and Sarah had finally arrived late Tuesday evening. Although all were exhausted, their eagerness to erase the time gap and the misunderstanding that had wedged between them overruled, and they'd spent several hours immersed in a lively and often soul-searching conversation. Finally, they succumbed to the need for sleep, and Mary showed them to the bedroom.

Her motherly instincts showing, Sarah asked, "Where will you sleep?"

"Don't worry Mama. The sofa makes a comfortable bed," Mary assured her. "Now you all get some rest. First thing in the morning, I'm going to the shop to see if Serena, my boss, needs me to work today. I'd already arranged to take today and the rest of the week off, but then I didn't go in yesterday.

Maybe you and Papa can come down to the shop and meet Serena—she's interesting."

"We'd love to meet your boss, but we don't want to cause you any trouble," Sarah replied. "Your father and I can take care of ourselves."

Mary looked into her mother's sweet face. She'd thought she would never see her Mama again, and now, here she was worrying about her as if Mary had never left.

"I love you, Mama," Mary whispered, as she wrapped her arms around Sarah. "You can't imagine how happy I am that you and Papa are here—and you are not causing me any trouble."

"I love you, too," Sarah replied, as she returned her daughter's embrace.

Mary closed the door gently behind her. Although sobered by the tragic events of the past few hours, her heart still overflowed with joy when she thought of her parents being a part of her and Jason's upcoming baptism and marriage. Deep in thought, she sighed, *If only Bryan could hear from his sister, Kathy.*

Please be with all those who are suffering and help Kathy and her son be alright, Mary prayed silently, as she looked up into the bright, blue Colorado sky. *And thank you again for being with my parents on their trip.*

The shop bell tinkled, and Serena looked up when she saw Mary enter. "Mary, I'm so happy you're here," she said, looking down at her scheduling book. "I'm having to rearrange everyone's schedule."

"Oh," Mary said, looking at Serena. Her long, straight, straw-colored hair hid her face as she continued to look at the schedule. She wore a long, full, flowery skirt and a loose-fitting linen tunic gathered at the waist by a turquoise and silver belt, which encircled her slender waist.

"I think she's only in her thirties, but she looks like pictures I've seen of the hippies back in the 1970s," Mary had told Jason when trying to describe her new boss.

Mary had been drawn to Serena's individuality and her artistic flair. When Mary and Jason had begun their Bible studies, Mary had eagerly shared what she was learning with Serena. Serena seemed interested and acknowledged that she watched a TV evangelist who taught the Bible the same way Mary was explaining it. Mary invited Serena to join them for the Bible studies and, for a while, Mary had thought she would come, but something always seemed to interfere.

"Is something wrong?" Mary asked.

"Well, it is this thing with your wanting off on Saturday. You've been working on Sunday instead, but we won't be opening on that day anymore," Serena answered.

"I see," Mary answered a little taken back. "Does this mean...?"

Looking up, Serena interrupted, "It means I think this group you're studying with has warped your thinking."

"But we talked. You made me think you agreed about Jesus's soon return and how keeping His Word was important."

"I told you I'd listened to an evangelist who taught that way," Serena replied. A smile spread across her face as she walked over to Mary and looked intently into her face. "I've been searching. Checking out different kinds of religions, and Mary—the most wonderful thing has happened!" Serena's face glowed, as the wonderful news gushed from her mouth, "I've found a teacher who introduced me to my spirit guide."

"Your spirit guide?" Mary questioned, trying to hide her bewilderment.

"Yes, he is helping me discover my inner power. He has shown me great truths. And," Serena's tone changed, "he has warned me about your group."

"My group?" Mary gasped.

"You are not keepers of the truth. You are dissenters—troublemakers. He says we must all worship as one—so that judgment will not come upon us."

"We must use God's Word as our guide—nothing else," Mary replied.

"But Mary, he has come to teach us all things and to deliver us."

"Who has come?" Mary asked.

Serena looked flustered, "I wasn't supposed to tell yet. It's the Messiah! He's here—the rock of our salvation, the cornerstone of our faith."

"What are you talking about?"

Serena's eyes flashed, "I'm talking about the Reverend Stone—his name refers to his being the rock. Can't you see it? You and your family, of all people, should know the truth since he healed your niece. How can you be so ungrateful?"

"But the Scriptures tell us that everyone will see His return."

Serena laughed, "Watch the evening news—you'll see him, and you'll see how wrong you are. One other thing—unless you change your mind, you are not welcome here."

"I'm fired?"

"It's your choice," Serena answered with a coldness that caused chills to run down Mary's spine.

"I see," Mary answered, as she turned and walked toward the door—away from the place where she'd spent so many happy hours working.

Sarah awoke to find Eli looking down at her. "Are you going to sleep all morning?" he teased her.

"Oh my, what time is it?" Sarah exclaimed, as she saw the morning sun streaming through the bedroom windows.

"I'll just say I'm glad I wasn't depending on you to do the milking," Eli said with a smile.

"We've only been away a few days, and you're already acting like a city slicker."

"What will Mary think?" Sarah said grabbing her robe.

"No rush, she's gone to the shop. She left us a note," Eli answered.

"I remember she said something about that last night," Sarah answered.

"I couldn't help but think of the other letter she left you when I saw this one on the table," Eli said solemnly, as he handed Sarah the note.

"That's in the past, and we'll not think of it anymore," Sarah replied, as she patted him on the arm.

They'd just finished cleaning up after breakfast when Mary returned. They listened quietly as she told them what had happened.

"I'm proud of you for walking away," Eli said. "If we are His followers, we must cling to His promises and hold on to His truth no matter what the consequences."

"How could the Reverend Stone fool so many?" Sarah questioned.

"It is the power given him by the evil one that is deceiving so many," Eli answered. "Jesus warned us about that in Matthew chapter 13, verse 19."

"Pastor Stanley says we are in a war between good and evil and that, for a time just before Jesus returns, it will appear as though evil as won, but that there will be a few who are faithful," Mary answered.

"The remnant, whom Satan went to make war on," Sarah added.

"Pastor Stanley calls us the Remnant People," Mary replied.

"We must ask God to give us the strength to remain faithful soldiers for His cause," Eli added.

"I wanted this to be a joyful time," Mary said, tears filling her eyes.

"It will be a blessed time, and that is what's important," Sarah answered, as she hugged her daughter. "The joy will come in God's time," she added. "Now let's talk about my daughter's wedding."

Mary brought out her wedding dress, fashioned with her own sewing skills.

"It's beautiful," said Sarah. "Simple, but elegant. I didn't know you were such a seamstress."

"You taught me well," Mary said, blushing at her mother's compliment. "I still want to take you out to lunch," she added.

They were getting ready to leave the apartment when an interruption in the earthquake coverage caught their attention. The cameras changed to the White House, as the President was introduced and began speaking. The Stoltzfuses listened quietly.

As the President finished, Eli said, "I wonder what he means when he says those who do not worship this Sunday will be dealt with as enemies of our country? It sounds as though he is categorizing those dissenters in the same group as terrorists and others who threaten our nation."

"And, if it is considered a wartime crime, there does not have to be an open trial by jury," Mary added.

"It's not any different from the CCC arresting Dr. Peter for not opening his office on Saturday," Sarah added, "and threatening us with arrest."

Eli agreed, "But it's the first time that to worship on Sunday has been made a national law."

Pastor Paul Stanley sat in the church study and quietly contemplated the President's speech and proclamation. He wondered, *Had the time come for them to close the church doors and go into hiding? The President hadn't said they couldn't worship on a day other than Sunday—just that they must worship on Sunday. What message would it send if they had worship on both Saturday and Sunday?*

He tried to think this through. *They could have their regular worship service on Sabbath morning, followed by the baptism of Mary, Jason, Bryan, and several others. Then, as the sun sank behind the Front Range, Jason and Mary would be wed. On Sunday, they would have a prayer vigil—they all certainly needed God's blessings. Perhaps that was the answer: obey the law if it didn't conflict with God's commandments.* Besides, how could he close the church doors when so many were coming to hear the Word. Each Sabbath, there were new faces in the congregation——so many so that he could hardly keep track of them all.

For a while, he'd wondered what was going to happen to the church as the membership kept dwindling. Pressure on Sabbath-keepers to abandon their convictions and join the false religious revival sweeping the country, combined with the prospects of civil lawsuits and job loss had caused many—some whom he'd considered the most reliable and faithful members—to join ranks with the dissenters. But, as times became more difficult, the remaining few became imbued with a holy boldness that Pastor Stanley had never before witnessed. He thought of Bev and Elizabeth and a dozen other young people who worked so tirelessly spreading the word. Their enthusiasm inspired the whole congregation.

Then there were others like Eli and Sarah Stoltzfus, whom God was leading—some through studying books that had been left in their homes years earlier. Others had discovered Bible truths through Internet programs or radio and television shows. Then there were those who'd had neighbors at one time who were Sabbath-keepers or others who knew about the church through its medical work. God's spirit was working in the hearts of His people. It was thrilling to see them searching for truth and a knowledge of God's Word and then to witness their enthusiasm as they shared it with others.

When he was younger, he'd sometimes wondered what the remnant church would be like at the very end. He was now seeing it for himself, and he now understood it wasn't the remnant church that was important, but the people of the remnant message who mattered. The church organization had already fallen apart in many aspects. It had first come under suspicion simply because it was a world-wide movement with humanitarian ministries in countries which had become blacklisted. The fact it kept politics out of the worship only appeased the authorities for a while. Worldwide political and social unrest, catastrophic national disasters, and the constant threat of attack by terrorists had drained the national budget and drawn the lines of scrutiny tighter and even more tightly around all non-profit organizations.

The church's refusal to change to Sunday worship had irritated the CCC leaders and had brought Sabbath worship to the attention of many. Others pointed to the fact that in the church's literature there were interpretations of Biblical prophecies about the role of America in the end-time events which were not very flattering.

The pastor, deep in thought, leaned back in his chair and clasped his hands behind his head. If only there were someone to talk to about all of this. Sadly, many of his colleagues in the ministry had left the church and, for a moment, he felt despair—but then he bowed his head and began to talk to his heavenly Father.

The sharp ring of the telephone startled him; how long had he been praying?

"Pastor?" Bryan's excited voice greeted him.

"Bryan, have you heard from Kathy?"

"Yes, Kathy has called twice. She and Kevin are alright and guess what?"

"What, Bryan?"

"Kathy and Kevin are going to stay with Mrs. Mattie until they can come here."

"Mrs. Mattie?" Pastor Stanley was trying to remember where he'd heard the name.

"You remember the lady who kept Kathy and me when we were children. The one who took us to church on Saturday with her."

"I remember," the pastor said. "That's wonderful."

"God is leading," Bryan added.

"I've no question about that Bryan. I'm looking forward to seeing all of you tonight and meeting Mary's parents."

As the pastor left the church, he wondered why so many people were milling around in the park across the street. His brow furrowed for a moment, and he wondered if there was cause for alarm when he saw a couple of men crossing the street and walking toward the church. His heart raced and his mouth felt dry. Then he heard a voice, soft and calm, but as distinct as if someone was standing beside him, "Go home. Don't worry. It will be alright."

He looked to see who had spoken. There was no one nearby, and he was puzzled but knew going home was the thing to do.

Chapter Seventeen

Asteroid

On Wednesday evening, Pastor Stanley went to Mary's apartment early, so he could meet her parents before the other members of the Bible study group arrived. She happily welcomed him, and then introduced him to Eli and Sarah.

Eli shook hands with the pastor and immediately liked his firm handshake and the way he looked him in the eye. As he and the pastor visited, the feeling continued. Eli sensed that here was a man who cared about people. They discussed how Eli had discovered the Bible truths and how it had led him to take a stand against the CCC. Eli observed the earnestness with which the pastor discussed his and Sarah's situation. Later, he would tell Sarah that there was something about Pastor Stanley that reminded him of Paul Jordan, the man who had sold them the Bible books, and Sarah admitted she'd had the same thought.

Bev, Elizabeth, and a couple of their friends, plus Bryan and Jason, arrived about thirty minutes after Pastor Stanley. Before prayer, the pastor addressed the group, "We have a lot to rejoice and thank God for this evening—Mary's parents, Sarah and Eli, have arrived safely and Bryan's sister and nephew were unharmed in the earthquake. But I also have some bad news to share with you. I waited until you were all here, so that I could tell everyone at the same time.

Movement in the room stopped, and every eye fixed on the pastor as he spoke. He continued, "This afternoon, after I left for home, the church was vandalized. The police said a Religious Unity Rally was being held in the park, and things got out of hand; one of the speakers singled out our church as being the stumbling block to unity and the cause of God's wrath. The perpetrators got into the church by breaking a window downstairs in the fellowship hall—everything is a mess in there. They tried to break into the church office, but I guess the police came before they managed to do that, so the copier and computer are okay. The biggest problem is that they turned on the fire extinguishing system, and there is a fine dust over everything, even in the sanctuary." The pastor shook his head and looked at Jason and Mary, "I don't know how we'll be able to meet in the building by Sabbath. We'll have to figure out some other place to have your baptism and wedding."

"That's not going to be so easy, is it?" Bryan asked. "That is with everyone thinking we shouldn't be worshiping on Saturday anyway."

Pastor Stanley replied. "You're correct. A few years ago, many of the Sunday-keeping churches would have been happy to help us, but I'm afraid that isn't the case anymore." He added, "God has an answer, I'm sure, so let's pray about it."

Other prayer requests were taken, and the group bowed in earnest prayer, thanking God for his blessings and asking for his wisdom in handling the new emergency. They did not finish until they asked God to forgive the vandals.

After prayer, Jason interjected, "I remember reading how worshipers in Communist countries formed cell groups and each group would meet in a member's home. Maybe we could divide into groups and do the same."

"But what about our baptism?" Mary asked.

Bev answered, "Years ago, my folks bought some land in a remote area in the high country—it's about seventy-five miles from here. We spent our summer vacations building a cabin. There's a creek running nearby. The water would be icy, but we could have a baptism and," she added, looking a Mary and Jason, "it would be a beautiful spot for a wedding."

"Would your parents mind?" Sarah asked.

"If they were here, they'd be pleased," Bev answered. "We thought the cabin would be needed for a time like this. It isn't fancy but there is a loft with extra sleeping room, and we've always kept a supply of canned foods and other non-perishable food in the cellar."

"If they were here?" Sarah asked, puzzled.

Mary explained, "Bev's parents went on a mission trip to Central America, and it's been six months since she has heard from them. There is a report that they were kidnapped by a rebel group."

"I'm so sorry," Sarah replied, looking anew at the young women who had brought God's message to her own daughter. Seeing the tears in Bev's eyes, she walked over and gave her a hug, "I've plenty of practice being a mother if you ever need someone to talk to."

"That's what God's Word does, it makes us all family," the pastor added.

They spent the next hour dividing the church members into groups, choosing leaders for the groups, and calling the leaders. The decision about where each group would meet would be left to the leader. The head elder volunteered to wait at the church Sabbath morning, so that if visitors came, they could be invited to a worship group. Assured satisfactory arrangements were made for the coming Sabbath, the group settled down for a heart-searching Bible study. "Please God, let it be your Word which guides us and not our preconceived ideas," was the prayer of each participant.

Mary shivered as she let the last guest out the front door. Though warm during the daytime, the evenings were beginning to be quite cool. "It could be cold in the mountains," she said to Jason, as she bade him goodnight. "We'd better pack some warm clothing."

Jason turned, the shadows intensifying the strong angle of his jaw, but Mary could hear the warmth in his voice. "Are you disappointed we can't use the church for the wedding?" he asked her.

"I think a high-country wedding will be just perfect," Mary said. "As long as the groom doesn't get cold feet!" she teased.

"After our baptism in an icy creek, we will probably both have cold feet, but our warm hearts are what matters," Jason replied. Then, in a more sober voice, he added, "Mary, I don't know what the future holds for any of us. I may lose my job when I refuse to work Saturdays. We may be put in jail if we don't go to church Sunday, but whatever happens, I promise you, I'll do my best for you."

"I know that Jason and, as long as we cling to Jesus, our best is good enough," Mary said, giving him a quick peck on the cheek.

"I love you, Mary Stoltzfus," he said softly, as he turned to go to his apartment. "See you in the morning."

Mary slept soundly that night. Visions of Jason holding her with towering snow-covered mountains as a backdrop and an icy stream gurgling at their feet filled her dreams.

At precisely eight o'clock, Thursday morning, September 9, regular television and radio programming were interrupted for an emergency press conference. A somber United States President, flanked by leaders of Congress, church representatives, and CCC officials filed onto the Capitol steps.

Cameras flashed and projectors rolled, as the President stepped to the podium.

"Fellow Americans," the President began. "Just yesterday I stood before you in order to assure you that the New Madrid earthquake disaster, though having the potential for a disaster, had not brought our country to its knees because we were prepared. I'm here to inform you of another potential disaster—not only to our nation but to all the people of this planet."

Mary had turned on the television to catch the latest update on the earthquake relief. She stood transfixed as she listened. Sarah and Eli, realizing that something momentous was happening, joined her in the living room.

The President continued, "I and these men who are with me have spent the past twelve hours conferring with top scientists and leaders the world over. All of them are conveying this same message to their citizens at this precise moment."

There was complete silence as the President paused and looked into the cameras, "A few weeks ago, an until-then unknown asteroid was discovered. After much research and analysis what we have feared for several weeks has now been confirmed. The asteroid is on a collision course and will hit the earth."

A gasp came from the audience, as they grasped the gravity of the words being spoken.

The President raised his hands to calm the group, "We are not without hope. According to all analysts, we have several weeks to act. Scientists and experts from around the world are—at this very moment—working on combining the most advanced technology we have in order to knock the asteroid off course. Those who are most knowledgeable about this technology will answer questions for you when I am through. We must remain calm and work together. There can be no looting or hoarding of goods. People who attempt to do so will be arrested. Each citizen must go on about his or her daily business. The most important thing to do is to pray. I have sought counsel with religious leaders in this country and with the Holy Father in Rome. We all agree. We must show a strong resolve to do the will of God. Yesterday, I pronounced Sunday as the official day of worship. Today, I have just signed an amendment to that bill which makes it illegal to worship on any other day. We are urging other nations to do the same. Those who disobey this mandate are enemies of this country and the people of the world. They will be treated as any other person

> *Yesterday, I pronounced Sunday as the official day of worship. Today, I have just signed an amendment to that bill which makes it illegal to worship on any other day*

who threatens national security. Their assets will be frozen, and they will be arrested. Each person listening must help us fight this evil, by keeping their eyes and ears open to detect those who are going against the law of this land and God's law. God's judgment is against us and we must show unity and allegiance to Him--our survival depends on it." The President stepped down, and the reporters began asking questions of the scientists.

"What should we do?" a white-faced Mary asked her parents.

"I think God has already shown us what to do when we were forced to make plans because the church was vandalized," Eli replied. Mary and Sarah shook their heads in agreement.

"What about Tom, Rachel, and Jonathan and their families?" Sarah agonized. "If only I could see them again and plead with Rachel and Tom to follow God's Word."

"The Holy Spirit will plead with them, but the decision to be a part of the true remnant has to be theirs. We cannot decide for them," Eli said.

"We can pray," Sarah and Mary said in unison.

"And God will listen," Eli replied.

The phone interrupted their prayer. Jason had heard the news. His co-workers on the construction crew were asking where he would be worshiping on Sunday. "It's getting ugly around here, so I'm going to quietly leave when I get a chance. I think we should go ahead and start for the cabin as soon as possible."

"Be careful," Mary said. "I'll call Bev and tell her about our plans."

Mary, Sarah, and Eli packed quickly, including warm clothing, sleeping bags, and extra food. Mary looked lovingly at her wedding dress as she placed it in a garment bag.

Two hours passed. They'd finished packing and made arrangements with Bev to meet her at the cabin. Mary paced the floor. What would she do if something happened to Jason?

"Things will be alright," Sarah assured her daughter. "God will watch over him."

At that moment, the door opened, and Mary ran to greet Jason.

THE WEBSTER FAMILY

Chapter Eighteen

Mrs. Mattie's Church

For Mattie Johnson, the decision to attend church on Saturday and go against the new Unity Law mandates did not occur on Thursday morning, September 9. That decision began long years ago when, as a child, she had given her heart to Jesus and been baptized one sunny, Sunday morning in the little country church that she and her parents attended. The decision deepened when she decided to leave that same church where she had grown up and to follow the new insight she had received from Bible studies with a man named Robert Drake. She'd gone to the pastor of her church and explained the things she was being taught. She'd asked questions about keeping God's law—all of it—including worshiping on Saturday, the seventh day. She'd not wanted to leave the church of her childhood and, as she questioned the pastor whom she'd known since birth, she waited for his answer and willed him to tell her that she was wrong so she could stay. But he'd sadly shook his head and said, "Mattie, we keep Sunday because of tradition. If you're not satisfied with that, then perhaps you do need to worship somewhere else."

Mattie had gone home and cried. But she had decided to follow Jesus, and that is exactly what she did. Her enthusiasm for the new truth she had found in the Scripture and her excitement to discover that Jesus's second coming was near had spread through the congregation of her church, and one-third of the members joined Mattie to worship on God's Sabbath. They met in Mattie's home. Thomas, her husband, had never gone to church, but he listened quietly to the group as they studied. Her biggest thrill was when he joined the little group and gave his heart to the Lord. After a while, they began construction on a church building not far from her home. Thomas worked tirelessly on the project and, it was one hot, August morning while he was helping with the roofing, that he had suffered a massive heart attack and, by evening, he was gone.

Mattie's one consolation was to know that Thomas had died in the Lord and one day soon she'd see him again.

After Thomas's death, it would have been so easy to blame God. The members of her former church dropped hints that, if she'd stayed where she belonged, Thomas would still be with her. Mattie knew better, and she didn't let them discourage her. She had made a choice to serve God, and—like the three Hebrews in the fiery furnace—if He slayed her, still she would serve Him.

So, her choice had already been made long before the President's speech. She listened, and then she turned to those who were with her and began to speak. "This is the thing we all knew would happen, and now it is the time for the world to choose whom they will follow. As for me, I will follow the Lord. On Saturday morning, I will attend church, as I always do. What you do is your decision, but I ask you to examine your hearts and to ask God to lead you."

"Couldn't we just worship here?" someone asked.

"You could," Mrs. Mattie answered. "But what are you going to do on Sunday—attend church? In the Bible, Daniel continued to pray in his window, as he had always done, even when there was a decree to kill those who prayed to gods other than Nebuchadnezzar. He could have prayed in his closet, but chose to be a witness. I choose to be a witness."

Kathy watched Mrs. Mattie as she spoke. She'd never heard her speak in such a clear tone. They'd studied together almost non-stop since she and Kevin had arrived yesterday. With the electricity out, it'd been too hot to sleep, so they'd sat on the big porch and listened to Mrs. Mattie explain the Scriptures. It was the same porch where she and Bryan had listened to Mrs. Mattie read *The Bible Story* books so long ago. The light from the oil lamp cast a soft glow on Mrs. Mattie's face and, as Kathy drank in the words, she thought again how Jesus must be a personal friend of Mrs. Mattie's. There on the porch, time sped by. The grandfather clock in the hallway ticked off the minutes and chimed the hours. The full moon sank below the horizon, and a thousand frogs croaked in chorus, as Kathy and Kevin gave their hearts to Jesus and vowed to be faithful to him. Kathy felt the burden of bitterness lift that she'd carried with her for so long, and she knew God had led Kevin and her to this place. They'd finally gone to bed and Kathy slept soundly.

The electricity came back on just as the President had begun to speak.

Kevin nudged Kathy, and she looked down at him. "We are going to church with Mrs. Mattie, right?"

"I...," she floundered for words and, reading the determined look on his face, she grabbed his arm.

"Do you know what this means?" she stammered, as he broke away.

"I know," he said, as he stood by Mrs. Mattie and looked into her kind brown face. "May I go with you to church on Saturday?"

"God bless you, child," Mrs. Mattie said, as she hugged him.

Kathy paused for only a moment and joined them, "Guess I'm going, too."

"Praise the Lord!" Mrs. Mattie exclaimed.

Others joined them, but some held back. "It's alright," Mrs. Mattie said, "You have until Saturday morning to decide."

It wasn't until Friday morning that Kathy remembered Kevin's birthday was the next day. She felt ashamed that she'd almost forgotten. When she mentioned it to Mrs. Mattie, her face lit with a smile. "Haven't had a genuine birthday celebration around here in a long time," she said, as she began rummaging through the pantry to see if she had the ingredients for a cake. Soon the cake was baking in the oven.

"I wish I had something I could give Kevin for a present," Kathy said. "He had such big plans for his birthday," she added, remembering how badly Kevin had wanted his dad to come.

"I have the perfect gift," Mrs. Mattie whispered to Kathy, as Kevin entered the room.

That night after supper, while they were enjoying Kevin's birthday cake, Mrs. Mattie came into the room carrying a large box.

"Didn't have any wrapping paper and these are not new, but your mother and I thought these would be the perfect present."

Kevin tore open the box and looked with delight at a whole set of *The Bible Story* books. "They are the books Mrs. Mattie used to read to Bryan and me," Kathy explained to Kevin.

"They are awesome," Kevin said, as he hugged his mom and Mrs. Mattie.

They spent the rest of the evening reading the books.

Chapter Nineteen

Jerusalem

In the country of Israel, on Saturday morning, at 9:00 a.m. (2:00 a.m. in Mississippi), a blinding light blazed momentarily over the city of Jerusalem and then, with dazzling brilliance, the Reverend Stone appeared. While most of the world watched, he proclaimed himself to be the returned Messiah. Like peals of thunder, his voice rolled across the city, as he urged the inhabitants of the world to repent and to rid planet earth of the evil ones who refused to obey God's laws. In cunning words, he explained why Sabbath worship was no longer necessary and how God's law had changed. "To worship me on Sunday—the day of my resurrection—is to show true unity with those who walk in my ways. My sheep hear my voice and will follow me," he quoted. "Again, I have come to save the world from the pestilence that befalls it. I plead with you do not turn me away." His voice broke at the appropriate time, and he hung his head and wept over Jerusalem.

Crowds had begun gathering at that great city after the announcement of the potential asteroid hit. They came because they considered Jerusalem a special place and were hoping for a miracle from God. They were not disappointed, and their voices rose in a mighty chorus as they chanted, "We will worship you."

While the remnant people were deep in prayer, asking for God's guidance and protection, most of the world watched the events unfolding in Jerusalem with rapt fascination. At last, they had hope—the answer was simple. Follow the "Messiah" and rid the world of those who refused to do so.

Chapter Twenty

Mrs. Mattie's Stand

Twelve hours later on a hazy Saturday morning in a small northern Mississippi community, Mattie Johnson got up and got ready for church—the way she always did. Three other families were staying with her, besides Kathy and Kevin. All but one person accompanied her on the short walk from her home to the little church. One couple, who had no children, walked beside Kathy and Kevin. Another family had a teenage daughter who had decided, almost as soon as Kevin and Kathy, to join Mrs. Mattie. Her father, concerned about his wife, who was not well physically, had hesitated, but they eventually both had decided that morning to take a stand with their daughter.

Leroy, a young man in his early twenties, walked with Mrs. Mattie, as he tried in vain to hide his tears. Margo, his wife, had refused to come. She'd held their baby tightly in her arms. "I've had enough of this craziness," she'd screamed at her husband. "I'm leaving. I'd rather stay in a tent than here." Leroy pleaded with her to choose what they both knew was right, but she refused and hurled more bitter words at him and the others. Mrs. Mattie placed her hand on Leroy's shoulders, "Let her go, son, you cannot choose for her," she said quietly.

"What about our baby?" he sobbed.

"God will restore the little one to you," Mrs. Mattie whispered.

They did not talk but resolutely marched toward the church. Kathy noticed the unusual silence. There was no traffic; no children played in the yards of the small frame houses they passed. Some had been damaged in the earthquake, but repairs had ceased. The silence was broken occasionally by the military helicopters which flew overhead.

"Had it been less than a week since the fateful night when their lives had changed forever? It seemed a lifetime ago," Kathy thought. She remembered how alone she'd felt on the walk to the armory, and she smiled when she

thought of how God had been leading her and Kevin all the time. He'd been there before that, intervening in ways she did not recognize until now. He'd allowed her and Bryan to become acquainted with Him and His Word when her parents had chosen Mrs. Mattie as their housekeeper. He'd given her strength when her parents died, and then again when Cal left. She thought of Cal and wondered what had happened to him. She wondered what would happen now to her and Kevin and the others with them? It didn't matter—they'd chosen to follow Jesus and to obey His commandments. Mrs. Mattie had called them the remnant people—the defenders of His Word. It sounded so noble, but Kathy knew she didn't have the resolve to stand alone and, only through the Savior's strength, would she overcome. Darkness had filled her with despair, but now she walked in the light of her Savior's love and acceptance. Mrs. Mattie's Jesus was now her friend also.

The church was the way Kathy remembered it, and memories overwhelmed her. She turned to Mrs. Mattie as they entered the sanctuary and asked, "Could we sing the song about Jesus's coming again? Bryan and I always liked that song. We even sang it to our parents."

Mrs. Mattie's faced gleamed, and she began to sing, and the others joined in. "Lift up the trumpet and loud let it ring, Jesus is coming again!"

Robert and Carol Drake walked into the church as the group began singing, and Carol went to the piano and began playing. They were singing their third song when the whine of sirens pierced the air, and the magnified voice of the county sheriff boomed against the walls of the church. "This is Sheriff Dawson; you are in violation of the Unity Law signed by the President on Thursday. Your church is surrounded. We'll give you ten minutes to come out with your hands over your heads, or we'll come in to get you." There was a pause, and the sheriff continued, "Now, Mattie Johnson, we know you're in there, and we don't want to harm women and children, so y'all just come on out and we'll talk about this."

Mrs. Mattie stood. She touched the rose-colored net which draped fashionably around the small-brimmed hat she wore. She smoothed her skirt. The others had not dressed up, and considering their circumstances, she understood why. But she'd always tried to look her best when she went to church, and today was no exception. She held her head high and walked purposely toward the front door. The others continued singing as they followed.

She stepped out into the bright sunlight and looked into the sheriff's face. "Brad Dawson, what are you doing here? Arresting the woman who used to teach you Bible stories right here in this church?"

Sheriff Dawson looked uncomfortable, "I know you're a good woman, Mrs. Mattie, but you're wrong about keeping the Sabbath. The Messiah is here, and last night he proclaimed the Sabbath commandment has been abolished and instructed us all to follow him. The world is on the verge of destruction, and asking him to forgive us and uniting with Him is our only hope."

Mrs. Mattie looked at her former student with compassion, as she began quoting scripture. Her voice resonated throughout the gathering crowd. "Now is the time to choose. Ask for His forgiveness. Accept His Sabbath. Obey His commandments. Turn your will and selfish desires over to Him. The time for your salvation is now."

"How much of this do we have to listen to," one of the deputies snarled.

Sheriff Dawson looked at Mrs. Mattie. Several spectators began agitating those around them, and they all began urging him to act. He hesitated for a moment, then squashed the impulse he had to join the little group on the church steps.

"Arrest them," he ordered. The crowd cheered. The lawmen raised their guns and rushed toward the church, as a low rumble began and the earth once more shook violently. The steeple on the church broke loose and toppled onto the onrushing crowd.

In the confusion, Mrs. Mattie and her group slipped into the church and escaped out the back door. They cautiously made their way back to Mrs. Mattie's home where they waited. During the ensuing days, her home would be surrounded by an angry mob several times.

Each time when the situation looked the most hopeless, the mob's eyes would be opened, and they would suddenly panic and run away, frightened by what had been— until now—an invisible armed host surrounding the home.

THE STOLTZFUS FAMILY

Chapter Twenty-One

In Lancaster County

Tom Stoltzfus folded the letter from Eli, placed it back in the envelope, then folded the envelope, and put it in his pocket. As hard as he tried, he couldn't forget his father's plea to study the Bible and to let God lead. He guessed he hadn't taken much time lately to study anything—not even his Bible. He'd been too busy being Thomas Stoltzfus, the firstborn son of Eli and Sarah Stoltzfus. What with him helping run the market and trying to be a good husband and a good church member, he never seemed to have a spare moment.

His brow furrowed. He was curious about the reason for his parents' unexpected departure. The market had not opened for two Saturdays now, and he wondered if the reason for their leaving was pressure from the CCC. The puzzling thing was he couldn't understand Eli running away—it wasn't like him. Rachel said she thought they'd gone to see Mary. Tom had been surprised to discover Rachel had been writing to Mary. And that Eli would go to see her—where was it she lived?—oh, yes, in Colorado—well that was surprising also.

Then he remembered Eli's talk with him that last night they'd been together. What had Eli said? That he, Eli Stoltzfus, was wrong, and he admitted that his refusal to listen to Mary had driven her from the family. Yes, there sure were a lot of unexpected things happening lately.

He felt the envelope in his shirt pocket. The morning was early, and the market had not yet opened. The business had been light with all the uproar about the Stoltzfus market closing on Saturdays. Still, there were faithful customers who kept coming. He was amazed about that, too. He hadn't expected so many to be sympathetic to Eli and his convictions. Even some of the Amish brethren had expressed concern and offered their encouragement.

Tom walked thoughtfully to his father's desk and opened the right-hand drawer. He'd seen Eli place a Bible there. He took the Bible and opened it. Where should he begin his search for answers? A slip of paper fell from the Bible, and he looked at the text written there. He turned to the first text and began reading. Besides that Scripture, a reference was written in Eli's handwriting. The clock ticked the minutes by. The assistant manager opened the doors to the store. Customers came and left.

Tom Stoltzfus was oblivious to anything happening around him as he drank in the Scriptures.

Jonathan and Amanda had been relieved to hear from Eli and Sarah. They'd agonized over the possibility that Eli and Sarah might have been near St. Louis when the earthquake hit. Since his parents' departure, Jonathan and Amanda had spent every spare moment visiting their neighbors. Among those they visited were the Martins, Pastor John Lapp, and Amanda's family who also remembered Grandmother's different beliefs. When he visited the pastor, Jonathan felt empathy for the man. The stress showed on his face, as he struggled between what—for all his ministry—he'd taught his congregation and the conviction that now he'd been wrong. The battle raged within, as the pastor wavered between what he now knew was truth and the temptation to keep the tradition of his people.

Jonathan kissed Amanda on the cheek as he sat down for lunch. "How's my wife and my little one?" he asked tenderly.

"We're both doing quite well," Amanda replied.

"I wish...," he said as he picked up his knife and spread a layer of butter across a thick piece of bread.

"Wish what?" Amanda questioned as she handed him the apple butter.

"I wish I'd had as much success with visiting Rachel as I've had with everyone else.

"What about Tom?" Amanda asked.

"Haven't been able to talk with him. He was gone Monday and Tuesday. I thought I'd call this evening—might even go by there."

The phone's ring interrupted their conversation. Amanda answered and handed it to Jonathan, "It's your brother," she said.

Rachel Zook paced the floor. She wished Jonathan would leave her alone. How could he let the madness that possessed their parents affect him also? And Amanda—she'd thought surely Amanda would do something to turn his thinking—the way James had done when she'd been tempted to go along with her parents. She was thankful for James and most of all for the Reverend Stone. Who knows what would have happened if he hadn't healed Julie?

Tires crunched on the gravel driveway, and Rachel looked up, startled. James came running in.

"Rachel, have you heard the news?"

"What's happened?" Rachel asked.

"The President has announced that earth is in danger of being hit by an asteroid." Rachel's face grew white. A ball of fear gripped her.

"What does it mean?"

"The end of civilization if it isn't stopped," James said. "There is hope if we unite."

"Unite?" Rachel questioned.

James explained the new amendment to the Unity Law.

"Neither my parents nor Jonathan will do it," she said flatly.

"Then they will be punished as traitors," James said.

"I know," Rachael replied, and she realized all affection she'd had for her family had vanished. In its place was a cold, hard anger.

The oppressive heat still lay heavy on the land Saturday morning in Lancaster County.

Dust swirled behind the cars which slowed and turned into the lane which led to Jonathan and Amanda Stoltzfus's home. Three Amish buggies soon joined the several cars parked by the farmhouse.

Jonathan and Amanda greeted each arrival with a heartfelt welcome. The Martins and two of their grown children were the first to arrive. Two cousins of Amanda's with their families soon joined them. To everyone's delight, Pastor Lapp came. There were others whom Jonathan did not know so well, but the news had spread that Jonathan and Amanda were opening their home Saturday to those who wished to follow the mandates of God, go against those of man, and worship on the true Sabbath. As they sang familiar hymns, another car pulled into the lane and Jonathan and Amanda greeted Tom at the door. Their hearts sank when they saw he'd come alone. Tom had begged Katie to come, but she had closed her heart to his pleadings.

There was no organized sermon or lesson study. They began with prayer. Like the disciples in the upper room before Pentecost, they were united in a desperate need for God's mercy and protection. They each poured out their hearts to the Savior whom they loved; it was because of that love that they had chosen to obey. When they finished praying, they sang and gave testimonies of how God had led them. Had it not been for the children among them, they would have forgotten to eat the lunches they brought with them—so intense was their worship. The day grew late and finally, with reluctance, they said their goodbyes. They were peaceful people, but they had defied the law of the land, and they did not know what would happen next. But like God's people through the centuries, the light of the Word burned within them, and no man could extinguish it.

Saturday afternoon a call was placed to the sheriff's office. "There is a group of Seventh-day Sabbath-keepers who are worshiping at the home of Jonathan Stoltzfus. These people are defying the President's Unity Law and endangering all of us," a young woman coldly explained.

Saturday evening, while most of Lancaster County slept, the order was given and—with the help of the local militia—those who had done nothing more than follow the dictates of their conscience were rounded up and confined in a temporary holding station until they could be sentenced.

Paul Jordan, Sabbath-keeper and seller of Christian books sat alone in his jail cell. For the past week, he had shared his cell with three others— two teens who'd been involved in gang-related violence, which they boasted about, and another older man, who'd been arrested for driving while intoxicated and endangering the life of a minor, his grandson. This morning, to their surprise, all three had been released. Paul heard voices and some commotion in the other cells, but he was too despondent to pay attention. His wife had died several years earlier, and he was glad she would be spared the heartache of seeing him in jail. He thought of his son and daughter; he'd cautioned them about what was coming, but they acted as if he didn't know what he was talking about. Now here he was, Paul Jordan, who'd spent most of his life ministering to others, alone and forgotten. The jail cell opened, and three men were pushed inside.

Tom Stoltzfus blinked his eyes trying to adjust to the dim light in the cell. He looked at the two others with him, John Lapp and Abraham Webb. He wondered if his face revealed the same quiet confidence that theirs did.

John Lapp spoke first, "They have taken our families, but they will not take our faith."

To Paul Jordan, the words seemed distant, and he wondered if he was dreaming, until he looked up and saw the three standing in his cell—a young man in his twenties and two others, one who was obviously Amish.

When he moved, Tom noticed the man sitting in the corner on the floor. He went to the man and knelt beside him. "Are you alright?" he asked.

Paul nodded. "Who are you and why are you here?"

"I'm Tom Stoltzfus, and this is John Lapp and Abraham Webb. Who are you?"

"My name is Paul Jordan," he spoke, as he struggled to get to his feet.

Tom looked at him. He'd heard that name somewhere before, and the man's face seemed vaguely familiar.

John Lapp spoke, "We are here because we have refused to disobey God's commandments."

"We are keepers of the seventh-day Sabbath," Tom explained, as he looked into the man's eyes.

The words registered slowly in Paul Jordan's thoughts. He looked from one to the other.

Tom's gaze had not left Mr. Jordan's face. He remembered a summer long ago when he was ten. A man had driven down their lane. A man who had a briefcase full of wonderful books.

That man had told Tom and the other members of the family stories from the books and then he'd prayed with them. Amish and Mennonite families spoke Pennsylvania Dutch in their homes and churches so Tom was not accustomed to hearing the "English" pray. So the man's appearance had stuck in Tom's memory. The books had arrived several weeks later, and that is when Eli had hidden the two adult Bible study volumes. Eli had said the salesman's name when he'd explained to the family the Bible messages he'd found by studying the books. The name was Paul Jordan.

Tom reached out to Mr. Jordan, "You came to my house and sold us Christian books. My father studied them with his Bible, and that is why we are here." His voice broke. "Thank you," he said, as he embraced Paul Jordan.

"If what Tom says is right, then we are also here because of you," John Lapp added.

The despair that had threatened to destroy Paul Jordan lifted. "God has not forsaken me. He has sent you here," he said incredulously.

THE REMNANT FAMILY

Chapter Twenty-Two

Waiting and Praying

The cool night air crept in through the cabin walls, and Sarah snuggled closer to Eli, thankful for the warm sleeping bags Mary and Jason had supplied. She thought of the three families camping outside and hoped they were as comfortable as she was. The window just above their bed framed a myriad of stars that seemed so close that she felt surrounded by their brilliance. She sighed; if not for the events unfolding around them, the day would have been perfect. The worship with the other believers had lifted her spirits. Near the cabin, a mountain stream tumbled and splashed its way downhill until it was captured momentarily in a small pool surrounded by giant boulders that had toppled across its path centuries earlier. It was here that they'd gathered for the baptism of Mary, Jason, Bryan, and two other couples.

Sarah's heart had overflowed as she watched Pastor Stanley immerse her daughter and the others in the cold pure mountain stream and then lift them out, symbolizing the death and burial of their old life and the birth of their new life in Jesus. She and Eli had committed themselves to following Jesus when they were young and had been baptized in their church, but, as she watched, she realized anew the significance. She whispered to Eli; he nodded his agreement, and together they approached Pastor Stanley. "We would like to be baptized again," Eli said as his voice broke. Pastor Stanley grasped their hands and led them into the cold mountain pool.

Afterwards, they had sat and watched as Jason and Mary were joined in marriage. Sarah could not absorb enough of the beauty surrounding them. She breathed in the crisp, pungent smell of the evergreens and observed how their shades of rich green framed the majestic, snow-covered peaks rising in the background. As Mary had stood there with her face aglow, Sarah had wanted to hold her—the way she had when she was small—and protect her from all the world's hurts, but now that was her husband's job.

Eli continued to rest peacefully beside her. What was going to happen to any of them she didn't know, and a shiver went up her back. The minutes ticked by; finally, Eli stirred.

"You awake?" he asked.

"Too much to think about to sleep, I guess," Sarah whispered.

"I've been thinking about our children. I wish I'd done a long time ago what I did today—take a stand for what I knew was the truth." He continued, "I don't know how God can forgive me for being so stubborn and not trusting Him."

"But He has," Sarah assured him. "Not any of us is perfect, but it's through His grace we will survive these last days and, in the end, stand in His presence.

"I don't know what I'd do without you, Sarah Stoltzfus."

"You'd do just fine as long as you had the Lord," Sarah replied.

The next morning dawned clear and still cool. Eli and Pastor Stanley started a fire in the wood cookstove. They looked through the supplies they'd brought and soon a hearty breakfast was underway. Jason and Mary appeared just as the food was being placed on the table.

"Can't sleep with all the noise going on out here," Jason explained.

"I guess you weren't planning on all of us spending your honeymoon with you," Bryan teased.

Mary blushed, "We are glad you all are here and thankful to Bev for providing a place for us."

The families that had camped came in, bringing food, and they all gathered around the table for the blessing.

They ate while discussing their situation. News had drifted in yesterday of the Reverend Stone appearing as the "Messiah; riots in the cities; talk of a death penalty for those who disobeyed the Unity Law—none of it was good news. The Reverend Stone was urging a global cleansing to rid the world of evil. "The death of evil will mean the survival of good," he'd cried in a thundering voice.

"Everyone is welcome to stay here until we are forced to go somewhere else," Bev offered.

"Thank you," Eli replied.

"I can't go home, so you know I'm staying," Elizabeth said.

There was more discussion. The families who had camped decided to hike further up into the mountains to a secluded place where they'd camped a few times before. Sarah worried about their children but was assured they were well equipped.

Pastor Stanley felt he needed to go back and try to assist others who might need his help finding a safe place to go. Maria, his wife, who was trying to hide her fears, kissed him goodbye and held her two small children tightly.

The four-year-old began to cry, and her mother consoled her, "Honey, I promise we will see Daddy soon."

Bryan took the six-year-old and promised to show him how to make a boat to float in the stream.

And so, the days passed. They rationed their food and prayed. The radio brought increasingly bad news. Groups of the remnant were rounded up and put in make-shift jails. A horrible disease, unparalleled in the suffering it caused its victims, was spreading throughout Africa and the Middle East. Along the Mississippi and its tributaries, fish were dying by the thousands. Scientists blamed it on pollutants from the damaged chemical plants and ruptured oil pipelines caused by the earthquake. The poisons had drained into the Gulf of Mexico and, on beaches from Mexico to Florida, the tide washed thousands of dead and decaying fish ashore. The eastern part of the United States continued to scorch under the intensified drought. The whole of Europe was plagued with the same problems and uncontrolled forest fires raged destroying everything in their paths. In China and Japan, devastating earthquakes had occurred. With each new problem, fear agitated the leaders of the nations and the religious powers to greater heights to cleanse the earth of those who refused to obey their mandates. Over all was the pall of coming disaster if the asteroid careening toward earth could not be shaken from its course.

Four days later, Pastor Stanley returned, and Sarah saw the joy on Maria's face. There was nothing more he could do for the ones who had been entrusted to him. Many had been captured; others had simply disappeared. He told of one of the older members who had given him shelter and hidden him in her attic, but then the militia had come and taken her away. He'd slipped away unseen later that night.

On the sixth day, helicopters flew low over the cabin. Eli was standing outside and heard them first. He'd signaled to the others, and they'd scampered inside, but he was sure they'd been detected. Several days earlier, Bev had taken him, Jason, and Bryan, further up into the mountains to a hiding place across the next valley where there was a small cave in the crevice of the rocks.

Several trails led away from the cabin, and they'd discussed how they'd divide and each take separate routes to the hiding place.

"Sarah, Mary, quick," Eli instructed as they grabbed the packs and headed for the back door, but the sound of jeeps winding up the trail told them that their efforts were too late. With one quick look at her parents, Mary turned and darted toward the front door. Jason followed her.

"Mary, don't," Sarah screamed, but it was too late. Bryan grabbed Sarah and Eli and pulled them through the door and into the nearby forest. As planned, Bev and Elizabeth ran down one trail, while the pastor and his family took another.

Sarah could hear shouting from the direction of the cabin. There was the loud retort of an automatic rifle and then a loud boom. From where they crouched, they could see flames shooting into the air and hear men cursing.

"Come," Bryan said, "This is our chance. Run!"

Sarah ran. Her chest burned with the exertion, as she gasped for breath in the thin mountain air.

She was thankful for the physical labor she'd done around their farm as her legs propelled her forward After a while, they slowed to a steady walk, always climbing up. After several hours, they crossed a boulder-strewn hill and looked down into a remote valley. Gray clouds were forming over the western peaks that rimmed the valley, and Bryan pointed across the valley to a rocky cliff.

"We're going there?" Sarah asked, not sure she could make it.

"We need to travel as far as we can," Bryan explained. "I don't know how much longer the weather will hold. It's a little early for a big snow, but I don't like the looks of those clouds."

"Where are the others?" Sarah asked.

Eli pointed to the right of them, "The trail the pastor took comes out over there."

"And Bev and Elizabeth should be somewhere below us," Bryan added.

They drank from their canteens and started down. Sarah was thankful for the sturdy boots and woolen socks Mary had given her, because walking downhill was more treacherous than their climb had been. She thought of sweet, loving Mary. She'd had her back for so short of time, and now she was gone. Her heart felt heavier than the pack she carried on her back.

Eli, reading Sarah's thoughts, whispered to her, "We'll be with her for eternity."

"I know," Sarah said, trying to wipe away her tears and keep pace with Bryan and Eli at the same time.

Rain began to fall in a steady drizzle about one-half hour after they caught up with Pastor Stanley and his family. The path they took was an animal trail, and it ran by a small stream that meandered through the valley. The ground was marshy because beavers had built a series of dams on the stream. They crossed over the top of one of the dams, sloshed through water up to their calves, and finally reached high ground. They'd put on their ponchos, but the rain still penetrated everything.

"It is a blessing though," Eli explained. "It'll wash away our tracks and smell and it is providing a cover for us from any plane."

"In fact, I doubt if they could fly in this weather," Bryan said.

Sarah shivered. Pastor Stanley looked at her with concern. "We've got to keep moving to keep warm," he cautioned.

After a while, they began climbing again. "We haven't seen Bev or Elizabeth," Sarah worried.

"I think they are waiting for us," Eli said, pointing up the trail to a crevice in an overhanging rock where a small fire flickered.

Sarah sat by the fire, thankful for its warmth. Although the opening in the rocks was small, the cave itself opened into a large room, and that surprised her. Later, after a prayer of thanksgiving for their deliverance and a plea for Mary and Jason's safety, they unrolled their bags and fell into an exhausted sleep. The next morning, they awoke to a white blanket of snow covering the ground outside. The snow had ceased falling, but the gray clouds still hung low over the mountains. They took down the food which had been hidden on the ledge, plus the few things some of the group had thought to grab as they rushed from the cabin. Then they asked Sarah to be in charge of the rationing.

Sarah looked over the meager amount. She knew it wouldn't be enough to sustain them for long.

Eli, seeing the concern on Sarah's face, gathered the remnant to pray for God to provide for them. Pastor Stanley reminded them of the ways that God had helped His people in the Bible, such as the manna sent from heaven to feed the Israelites and the ravens that brought food to Elijah. The remnant prayed fervently, as they pleaded for God's help, each person remembering instances in the past when God had miraculously watched over him or her. When they finished praying, Sarah, with the others helping, separated the food into small amounts for each day. As they handed out the day's supplies, she wondered if there would even be enough for the next day.

The next morning, she arose early to see what food was left and, to her amazement, there was more remaining now than there had been before they had handed out food the previous morning! It was clear that God was providing for this remnant group. And so they waited.

Throughout the earth, the remnant waited. Waited in crowded jail cells, in dark caves, in desert places, or in wilderness hideaways. Some were with other believers, but they were all alone—lost in their thoughts. Memories haunted them. A recollection of past mistakes flashed through their minds. Each person was acutely aware of their unworthiness, and it threatened to overwhelm them. In their desperation, the beautiful promises of God's Word sustained them as they clung to Him, pleading for His grace. They waited while—like a monster loosed from its chains—the bands of law, order, and civility stretched and broke. Triggered by fear and propelled by hatred, the wrath of the masses was turned against those who refused to obey earthly demands.

> *Throughout the earth, the remnant waited. Waited in crowded jail cells, in dark caves, in desert places, or in wilderness hideaways*

The rumbling awakened Sarah. She lay still trying to decipher where the sound came from. Her heart pounded, as she thought it might be the helicopters they each feared. Helicopters would bring armed, angry men who despised them for refusing to let go of their beliefs.

She turned to find Eli and saw that he was already up. She struggled to her feet and walked with him to the cave entrance. A strange gray-green light filtered through dark, angry clouds. Flashes of lightning split the heavens, as thunder echoed across the mountain peaks. A marmot, whom Sarah had tried to make friends with, chattered excitedly atop his craggy home.

A sudden gust of wind pushed Sarah backward, and she reached for Eli's hand. The others joined them at the cave entrance. The ground trembled beneath their feet. Huge boulders broke loose and thundered down the mountainside. Sarah shuddered.

"God is our refuge and strength, a very present help in trouble," Eli began to quote Psalms 46. Others in the small group of believers joined him. "Therefore will we not fear, though the earth be removed, and though the mountains be carried into the midst of the sea."

Chapter Twenty-Three

He Comes!

Suddenly the heavens part, and a brilliant light pierces through the gloom. A living cloud, indescribable in its glory, fills the heavens and encircles the earth. As the inhabitants of earth watch, every heart burns with the precepts of God's law. The remnant watch in awe, while those who had disregarded His commands tremble with terror and try to hide from the glory of Jesus's return. From its foundation, the earth shakes. Volcanos erupt. Buildings crumble. Graves open, and all those who had been redeemed through the ages are raised from the earth to meet their Redeemer in the air.

As Sarah, Eli, and thousands of the faithful remnant around the world gaze into that beautiful, shimmering light, joy fills their hearts. The darkness is gone!

With one voice throughout all the earth, the redeemed shout together joyously, "Lo, this is our God; we have waited for him, and he will save us."

Then each one hears Jesus speaking, His voice deep and melodious, "Come! You who are harmless and undefiled. You have kept the word of My patience. You have been faithful and true. You shall walk among the angels and receive a crown of glory." And, as the mountains give way beneath their feet, all of those who are alive—and have remained faithful through persecution—join the redeemed of all ages to meet their Savior in the air to forever be with Him!

Amen and amen!

* * *

The characters in this book are based on people the author has met. The end-time events are based on prophecies found in the Old and New Testaments of the Bible.

If you would like to discover more about these biblical prophecies, please contact the address below for free Bible study guides:

Find Peace, Power, and Purpose for Your Life!

amazingfacts.org

Enroll in our FREE online Bible study course and discover:

- What happens after death
- The way to better health
- How to save your marriage
- The surprising news about hell
- Why the Bible is relevant today
- The "mark of the beast"
- Who really gets "left behind"
- ... and much more!

Or enroll in the postal mail course! Send your name and address to:

AMAZING FACTS
P.O. Box 909
Roseville, CA 95678

27 full-color, illustrated, Scripture-packed, easy-to-understand lessons!

TEACH Services, Inc.
P U B L I S H I N G

We invite you to view the complete
selection of titles we publish at:
www.TEACHServices.com

We encourage you to write us
with your thoughts about this,
or any other book we publish at:
info@TEACHServices.com

TEACH Services' titles may be purchased in
bulk quantities for educational, fund-raising,
business, or promotional use.
bulksales@TEACHServices.com

Finally, if you are interested in seeing
your own book in print, please contact us at:
publishing@TEACHServices.com

We are happy to review your manuscript at no charge.